Love Is a Four-Letter Word

by **VIKKI VANSICKLE**

Scholastic Canada Ltd.

Toronto New York London Auckland Sydney
Mexico City New Delhi Hong Kong Buenos Aires

For Rebecca Jess, who believes in love;
and for Tiffany Clayton, who found it.

Scholastic Canada Ltd.
604 King Street West, Toronto, Ontario M5V 1E1, Canada

Scholastic Inc.
557 Broadway, New York, NY 10012, USA

Scholastic Australia Pty Limited
PO Box 579, Gosford, NSW 2250, Australia

Scholastic New Zealand Limited
Private Bag 94407, Botany, Manukau 2163, New Zealand

Scholastic Children's Books
Euston House, 24 Eversholt Street, London NW1 1DB, UK

Library and Archives Canada Cataloguing in Publication
VanSickle, Vikki, 1982–
Love is a four-letter word / Vikki VanSickle.

ISBN 978-1-4431-0787-7

I. Title.

PS8643.A59L68 2011   jC813'.6   C2011-902458-6

Cover image: bodhihill/istockphoto

6 5 4 3 2 1   Printed in Canada 121   10 11 12 13 14

Hope

Is there anything more depressing than the end of March Break? Easter fell early this year so I don't even have that to look forward to. Now it's one big, long endless stretch until the Victoria Day weekend in May. These are the disturbing thoughts that run through my mind, waking me up at some ungodly early hour on a Saturday morning, my second-last day of freedom. I haul myself up on my elbows and listen for any signs of life, but it doesn't sound like Mom is up yet. So why should I drag myself out of bed?

I turn over my pillow, punch it back into shape, and settle back down into the comforter. Before long I am happily on my way to sleep, daydreaming about giving an exclusive interview on my latest award-winning performance, when an alarm starts to go off. It's distracting me and the perfectly styled reporter in front of me, who keeps looking over her shoulder.

"Clarissa! The phone!"

Why does the reporter sound exactly like my mother? And why won't that ringing stop? Where is my personal assistant? Where is the producer of the show? What kind of TV show is this, anyway?

"Nobody I know would call at this hour."

1

Mom again. And the ringing is getting louder. And then it dawns on me. There is no reporter, no interview. I'm dreaming. That awful noise is the phone. Talk about a rude awakening. Now that I know what the sound is, reality comes crashing around me and the dream that just seconds ago felt so real vanishes. I fling an arm out of the covers and fumble around for the phone, keeping my eyes closed, as if that will keep the last bit of the dream trapped in my head. Finally my hand connects with the phone.

"Yes?" I meant to say hello, but I've never been much of a morning person.

"Clarissa! Guess what?"

Of course. Benji. My own personal rooster. If I believed in things like past lives I would swear on my life Benji was one of those birds that starts squawking in the dark of the morning before the sun comes up.

"What time is it?"

"I don't know, maybe eight-thirty? Were you asleep?"

"Benji, it's Saturday. Most normal people are still asleep."

"Oh, sorry." For a moment Benji sounds guilty but he shakes it off quickly enough. "Can I tell you why I was calling?"

"Go ahead," I mutter.

"I was reading the paper this morning and there's something I think you should see on page four."

That's another thing about Benji. How many thirteen-year-olds do you know who read the paper? Even if it is only the local, sappy eight-page paper?

"Can't you just tell me what it says?" I ask.

"No, I want you to read it. It'll be more fun! Aren't you even a little curious?"

I have to admit, I am just a little bit curious. Benji is an early riser and everything but he knows better than to wake me up before I'm ready. Whatever he found on page four must be something big.

"I don't even know if we get the paper," I complain.

But Benji has the answer to that already. "Everyone gets the Saturday paper; it's free. It's probably still on your doorstep."

"Fine." I manage to pull myself up and swing my legs over the edge of the bed. "I'm up."

"Okay, go get it and call me right back. Call me before you open it."

"Okay, okay. Bye, Benji."

Mom is still in bed, reading, when I pass her room on the way to the front door. "Benji?" she asks, without looking up from her book, something cheesy about a housewife and a marine, probably supplied by Denise, her best friend and bearer of bad books and good cosmetics.

"Who else?" I reply.

Sure enough, just as Benji predicted, *The Bugle* is sitting on the welcome mat outside the front door. The Booger is more like it. I grab it and head for the kitchen table.

I guess I should be happy that I live in a small town with a paper full of local stories instead of pages and pages of war and crime. But I have to wonder, do the people of Toronto or Vancouver or New York City have to wake up and see a story on the front page of their papers about a woman who made it into the *Guinness Book of World Records* for having the largest collection of Precious Moments figurines? Probably not. When I'm famous, I wonder if they will print front-page articles about me. That'll be a nice change for the people of this sad little town.

I turn to page four. At first I don't see anything, just a

3

story about a sports team, a column about an alumni event at the high school, and a bunch of ads. Then I see it, a small notice buried in the advertisement section:

> **Think you've got what it takes to be a star?**
> *The Gaslight Community Players are looking for actors between the ages of 12 to 18 for our youth presentation of the classic musical* The Wizard of Oz. *No prior experience necessary! Auditions on Saturday, 4 to 8 pm.*

***

Fifteen minutes later Benji and I are sitting on the kitchen floor, staring up at the audition notice that is now on the fridge. I'd cut it out of the paper and rearranged the magnets so the only thing on the freezer is the notice; new hope on a clean slate. I keep re-reading the ad, just to be sure I've got all the details right. For as long as I can remember, I have loved *The Wizard of Oz*. I have also always felt that I was destined to be an actress. And here is an ad, telling me I can combine my love for the Wizard and my secret desire to be an actress? It's almost too good to be true.

"Are you going to audition?" I ask.

Benji shrugs. "I don't know, I was thinking maybe I could help with costumes." Benji loves *The Wizard of Oz* almost as much as I do. If only he wasn't so shy.

"You should audition," I urge him.

"I don't know if I can sing in front of people," he says.

"You sing in front of me," I point out.

"That's different," he protests. "These are strangers. Plus they'll be listening to people all day long who are ten times better than me."

4

"I think you have a nice voice."

"Thanks," says Benji. "I'll have to think about it. What would I sing?"

"Whatever you want . . . Maybe not 'Over the Rainbow,' that's a girl song."

Benji thinks about it for a minute. I can tell because he's chewing his lip. He always chews his lip when he thinks. "I could sing 'O Canada'," he says. "At least I know all the words to that."

"Perfect! Let's practise." I jump up but Benji stays put, staring at the fridge.

"Maybe I'll just stick with costumes. I like costumes."

"I think you should go and if you chicken out you can just sign up for costumes."

Benji frowns. "I'm not chicken," he says.

I grin. "Then prove it."

Wait

"This is so exciting! I'm so proud of you guys, auditioning for a big musical! Wow, there sure are a lot of people here! Are you nervous? Don't be nervous."

The only reason I invited Mattie Cohen was to keep Benji's spirits up while I was inside auditioning. I practically had to drag him out of the house and I know that if left to his own devices he would worry himself into a state and never go through with the audition. So Mattie agreed to come along to keep him distracted. Only now she's getting on my nerves.

"I think it's smart to wear your hair in braids, it makes it easier for the audition panel to imagine you as Dorothy. Oh, Clarissa, you'd be a great Dorothy!" Mattie squeezes my hand. It's amazing what a strong grip she has.

"Okay, okay, calm down," I mutter. "People are staring."

I'm surprised how many people are here. A lot of them look older, like high school students. They've probably done all sorts of musicals before. I try not to think about that.

Benji is looking a little pale.

"Are you okay?" I ask. He nods, but doesn't say anything. Instead, he starts riffling through the portfolio of costumes he's created to present in case all else fails and his voice or nerves give out.

"Okay, so it looks like we have to go sign up at that desk over there and then wait to be called," Mattie says. "Come on, let's go."

Mattie marches up to the desk and offers her hand to the woman working behind it. "Hello, my friends here would like to sign up for an audition."

"And will you be auditioning as well?" the woman asks. She's wearing earrings in the shape of drama masks.

Mattie titters. "Oh, no. I'm just the fan club."

Now they both laugh. The woman's drama masks jiggle. "I wish *I* had a fan club! My name is Carol. I'm on the board for the Gaslight Community Players. Have either of you auditioned for us before?"

I shake my head, no. Benji appears to be unable to move.

Carol hands us each a form. "Well then, I'll need you to fill these out and bring them back to me. We have a bit of a backlog at the moment but I can fit you in at seven-ten and seven-twenty. How does that sound?"

"Perfect!" Mattie chirps. "Thank you, Carol."

It's only six-thirty. I'm not sure I can handle sitting around for that long with nothing to do but worry. Mattie finds us a corner and we all sit down and look over the forms. Past shows? Dance experience? Vocal range? The butterflies in my stomach are migrating toward my throat, which can't be a good thing, considering I have to sing in less than an hour.

Benji looks even worse than I feel. "What does vocal range mean?" he whispers.

"I don't know," I admit. "Maybe they want to know what kind of songs you can sing?"

Benji frowns. "That doesn't sound right."

"Maybe put down average? You can't go wrong with average." So we both write "average" under vocal range.

"What are you going to put for dance experience?" Benji asks.

"Have you ever taken dance classes?" Mattie says.

"No, well, just that time we did line dancing in gym class. But I don't think it counts."

"Everything counts!" Mattie insists. "Write it down! What about past shows?"

"I was in a play in grade three," Benji says. "We both were, Clarissa. Remember?"

"Do you mean the one where we dressed up as pioneers?"

"I remember that!" Mattie cries. "'Yonder Years'!"

How does she remember this stuff?

"You could put down the radio show, Clarissa," Mattie suggests.

"I don't know, that's not the same thing as acting in a play."

Mattie shrugs. "At least you won't have to leave it blank," she points out.

So I write "host of exciting radio program." That's not exactly a lie.

Someone is singing scales in the stairwell. She sounds really good, especially on the high notes. Her voice gets even stronger as she gets higher. My high notes get more and more wobbly as I go up. My throat is starting to feel dry. Good thing Mattie told us to bring water bottles. I down half the bottle, a little too quickly, spilling water down my chin and across the front of my shirt. Wonderful.

Benji is starting to get fidgety. It's making *me* fidgety. If I don't find a way to distract him, both of our auditions will suffer and this year will be the same as any other boring year and I will have lost my chance at stardom. I've pictured myself on stage for so long, and here I am with the perfect opportunity. And in *The Wizard of Oz*, no less — my all-time favourite book, movie, and now musical!

"Hey, Benji, why don't you show Mattie your sketches?"

Mattie beams. "Oooh, yes please! I'd love to see them!"

Mattie bounces over and squeezes herself between us. Normally I'd be annoyed but it's good to have a whole other person between me and the bundle of nerves that my best friend has become. Benji relaxes as he explains each of his costume designs. Mattie asks all sorts of questions and makes just the right kind of noises.

Every five minutes, a woman with a clipboard and a bad perm steps into the hallway and calls a name. The chatter freezes and everyone watches as someone gathers their belongings and heads into the gym. Then there's the muffled sound of a piano and people go back to what they were doing. Even though I know it's not helping, I can't stop checking my watch. Six-forty, six-forty-five, six-fifty. How can things be moving so slowly?

"Charity Smith-Jones?"

Someone gasps and Mattie clutches the sleeve of my nicely pressed Dorothy-esque blouse in her hand. "What did she just say?" she hisses in my ear.

I don't have to respond, because the woman clears her throat and says a little bit louder, "Charity Smith-Jones? Is Charity here?"

Just then the door to the stairwell swings open, narrowly missing Benji, and the girl with the great high notes strolls out. She has the most beautiful long, red hair I have ever seen, just like Ariel's from *The Little Mermaid*. It's long and full and spills over her shoulders in the kind of loose waves that can only be achieved by high-quality hot rollers. My mom's best friend Denise would be so jealous. She has been dyeing her hair red for years.

"Sorry, Bev, I was practising," Charity trills.

The woman (Bev, apparently) looks absolutely charmed. "Don't worry, Charity, we're just happy to see you here. We thought after those commercials we'd lost you for good."

Charity laughs. Even I am enchanted. "Oh, Bev! You know I could never leave the theatre!"

Mattie lets out a great gush of air as the door shuts behind Charity and Bev. "Do you know who that was?" she asks breathlessly. "Charity Smith-Jones!"

"Yes, I heard, Mattie."

"But do you know who she *is*? She's in grade ten at Sir John A. and has been the lead in every musical, even when she was in grade nine. She also does commercials. She's the girl from the Tim Hortons commercial — you know, the Roll Up the Rim one?"

Benji gasps. "I know the one you mean! The one with the girl in the pink earmuffs! She uses her allowance to buy her mom a coffee and it ends up being a million dollar cup! SHE'S THE GIRL IN THE PINK EAR MUFFS!"

Leave it to Benji to remember her ear muffs.

"Do you remember it, Clarissa?"

Of course I remember it. Everyone knows that commercial. It plays every single commercial break. Charity Smith-Jones must be a millionaire by now.

"Do you think she's going for Dorothy?" Mattie asks.

I shake my head. "No way, her hair is too distinctive. Dorothy has brown hair."

"But what if they have wigs?" Benji says.

I shoot him a look. Benji cringes. "On second thought,

it's just a community show, they probably can't afford wigs," he says.

I won't believe it, I can't. This is my part. I will not give it up to a red-haired TV star. I remind them that in the movie Glinda has red hair. Benji and Mattie nod.

"You're so right!"

"She'd be the perfect Glinda!"

"You know who else she could play?" Benji says. "Not in this show, but in another one?"

Mattie and Benji look at each other and blurt out at the exact same time, "Anne of Green Gables!"

Mattie sighs wistfully. "She'd be the perfect Anne." She adds, catching my eye, "And Clarissa would be a divine Diana."

"Diana's hair is black," Benji points out.

"Maybe they have wigs!" I say, perhaps a bit too savagely.

Bev reappears in the doorway. "Clarissa Louise Delaney?"

This is it. I manage to get to my feet and make it to the door, clutching my form. Charity breezes past me, all smiles and dimples and perfect hair.

"Break a leg," she says.

Easy for her to say.

Sing

Inside the auditorium, the murmur of the hallway disappears. It's totally silent, like a church or a tomb. I walk down the centre aisle to the front of the room, near the stage, where not one but five people smile at me as I approach. They are seated around a table littered with stacks of paper, coffee cups, water bottles, and a Timbit party pack.

"Who do we have here?"

I swallow, clearing what feels like the world's biggest cotton ball from my throat and manage to say, "Clarissa Louise Delaney."

Why am I nervous? I shouldn't be nervous. I've done things that are much harder, like visit my mom at the hospital, or yell at Terry DiCarlo, or spend two whole weeks with Denise, but for some reason I can't stop my heart from jumping all over the place. One minute it feels like it's in my throat, the next it's in my stomach. I can even feel my pulse throbbing in my fingertips.

"How are you today, Clarissa?"

"Fine, considering."

"Considering what?"

"Considering I have to sing in front of strangers." The audition panel chuckles. I feel a little bit better. A sense of humour is a good thing, right?

One by one they introduce themselves to me: Karen, the director; Brian, the music director; Nadine, the choreographer; Becky, the assistant director; and Nelu, the accompanist.

"Accompanist?" I repeat.

Nelu smiles at me. "I'll be accompanying you, on the piano. Did you bring sheet music?"

I shake my head, no. "Was I supposed to?"

"No, no," says Brian the music director. "We'll just get you to sing a cappella and do a range test."

The words "range test" send my heart plummeting to the bottom of my stomach. I'm not entirely sure what it means, but I've never been good at pop quizzes.

"Do you want to start with a scene or your song?" Karen asks me.

"Scene," I say quickly. The longer we leave the singing, the better. Plus this way I can wow them with my acting abilities and they'll be willing to overlook my singing. Not that it's bad but it's not exactly great, either.

Karen, the director, is smiling at me. She hands me two sheets of paper. "Great! I'm going to ask you to read two scenes. The first one is when Dorothy meets the Scarecrow. Nelu will be reading the part of the Scarecrow."

Nelu smiles at me again. She has friendly eyes and very white teeth. I decide I like her the best.

"Would you like a minute to read over the scene?" Karen asks.

"No, I'm ready," I say. The thought of standing there reading to myself while the whole audition panel stares at me is not appealing. Besides, I've seen *The Wizard of Oz* at least a hundred times. I could probably recite the whole scene by heart.

"Whenever you're ready," Karen says.

I take a deep breath, remind myself to speak slowly and clearly, and begin the scene. At first, my voice is a little shaky and it's hard to look up from the script, but by the time we get to the end I can hear my voice, clear and strong, bouncing around the auditorium. It's an awesome feeling, very powerful.

When I finish, the audition panel claps politely before scribbling madly in their secret books and on pieces of loose-leaf paper. What I wouldn't give to sneak a peek at their notes!

"Very nice, Clarissa. Next I'm going to have you read for Auntie Em," Karen tells me.

I almost choke on my own saliva, or what's left of it in my dry, nervous throat. "Isn't that part more for older kids?"

Karen smiles, but her expression is hard to read. I recognize that kind of smile — my mother is a master of the impossible-to-decipher Mona Lisa smile. "Traditionally, yes, but this is a youth cast so we'll have young actors playing roles of all different ages. You never know, you might be the perfect Auntie Em, or Tin Man."

"The Tin Man's a boy," I protest.

"The Tin Man is whoever we want him to be," Karen corrects me. "Boys might play girls, girls might play boys. At this point it's wide open. That's what's so exciting about theatre — expect the unexpected."

"So, Dorothy could be played by a boy?" I ask.

"Maybe!"

I highly doubt that, but given that Karen is the one making decisions, I don't want to get on her bad side, so I fib a little. "That's cool."

Karen beams. "Wonderful! Now let's see what you've got for Auntie Em."

So I read the part of Auntie Em. I admit, my heart isn't really in it. I just can't get into the role. Her lines are so boring — "No, Dorothy" this and "poor Toto" that. When I finish, the panel claps again and Brian asks me what I'm going to sing.

"'Over the Rainbow,'" I say. Suddenly I feel a little foolish. I bet everyone sings "Over the Rainbow." Maybe another song would be more memorable, or at least a change of pace. Now I will be compared to every single girl who sang "Over the Rainbow" before me. Oh, well, too late to change now.

"I probably would've picked it even if I wasn't auditioning for *The Wizard of Oz,*" I say. "I really like the song."

Brian winks at me. "Me, too. It's a classic. Do you need Nelu to give you a starting note?"

I shake my head, no, and silently curse my mother for never putting me in piano lessons. I could be halfway to being an opera star right now instead of floundering around like a fish out of water, a fish who wouldn't know what note to start on if you gave her the choice of notes to pick from.

I have to clear my throat two times before I start, but when I sing, I think I sound all right. I look over the heads of the audition panel into the empty auditorium. It dawns on me just how many seats are in here. As I wonder whether or not I could sing in front of a full house, my voice wavers a bit. I decide to look over the audience and into the balcony, at the back windows. I imagine I'm looking for a rainbow, or at least a bluebird.

When I finish, my cheeks are flushed and I am feeling pretty proud of myself. The panel claps again and Brian leans over and says something to Nelu, who gets up and goes to the piano.

"Very nice, Clarissa. Now if you don't mind, we're going to get you to sing it again in a different key," he says pleasantly.

"Key?" I repeat.

Nelu's fingers spread over the piano and she plays a chord, followed by a single note. "Can you sing this note?" she asks.

I open my mouth and try to match my voice to the sound coming from the piano. It sounds right, although it's just a little higher than I like to sing.

"Good," Nelu says. "We're going to sing it again, and this time I'm going to play with you. Just follow along with the piano."

She makes it sound like the easiest thing in the world, but the song is much faster than I remember, and too high. My voice gets thin and reedy and I can't seem to take in enough air to get through all the words. Soon I'm caught between whisper-singing and gasping for air. When we finish, my breathing is ragged, like I've just run the four-hundred-metre dash, sprinting the whole way. I'm so embarrassed I want to crawl under a rock and die — but I can't, because I still have to do something called a range test.

The panel claps again, but this time it seems insincere, their smiles phoney. They probably have to clap after every person, no matter how good or bad they are. Nelu talks me through the range test, but my ears are buzzing and I'm try-ing so hard not to cry that I barely hear the instructions. She plunks notes and I follow along, trying to squeeze out the notes between the lumps that have formed up and down my throat.

When it's over, Karen says something about a list and callbacks and thank you very much for coming, but I can tell by the way she is smiling indulgently at me and the pity in Nelu's eyes that I will not be getting a call. The effort of holding back my tears is enormous, and starting to burn my throat. Images of my entire life, the life that I was meant to lead, flash before my eyes: me bowing on stage while fans throw roses at my feet; me at my first premiere; me on Oprah; me getting my first Oscar. They all disappear like words in the sand, washed away by the tide.

Karen gets up to shake my hand and I smile weakly before turning and getting the heck out of there as fast as I can without running.

Fine

When I get back, Mom and Denise are giggling over something in the kitchen. It's embarrassing to hear a grown woman giggle, especially your own mother.

"What's so funny?" I ask.

Mom beams at me. "There she is! Future superstar and multi-award-winning actress! Well, how did it go?" She pulls me close to her and tugs on the end of one of my braids. "Nice touch," she adds.

"Thanks."

Next she starts unbraiding my hair and running her fingers through it. I let her do this, even though I'm getting too old for it, because she lost all her hair a few months back. Just over a year ago, my mom was diagnosed with cancer. She's had three treatments and the doctors say things are going "according to plan" — which is good news — but no one is saying the magic word *remission* just yet. But the minute they do, Denise says, "We're throwing your mama the biggest remission party there ever was!"

Denise is big on parties, as long as they aren't in celebration of her birthday. For as long as I can remember, Denise's birthday party consists of a cake that says, "twenty-nine again!" and a bottle of wine that she shares with my mother in front of the TV. Pretty lame if you ask me.

She never says anything about it, but I know Mom misses having her own hair. My mom is a former beauty queen and a very successful hair stylist. Hair is everything. Some people would say that life is everything and of course they're right, but they probably never had their hair fall out.

At first, Denise taped pictures of Halle Berry and all sorts of actresses with really short hairstyles to the mirror in the bathroom. Now that her hair is starting to grow in, Mom looks just as good as any of them. She says she loves the no-fuss look, but last week I found her old straightening iron and hot rollers in the garbage. I think it made her sad to see them every morning in the bathroom, knowing she won't be able to use them for a long time.

"Come on, kiddo, don't keep us waiting. We're not getting any younger," Denise says.

"It was fine," I say carefully.

"Fine?" Denise repeats.

I shrug. "Yeah, fine."

Mom kisses my neck. "I'm sorry, sweetheart," she says.

I twist away from her. "Sorry for what?" I demand. "I said it was fine!"

"Okay, okay!" she says. "Take it easy! You just sounded a little down. But if you say it went fine, then great. I'm glad."

"Your first audition, you deserve a treat!" Denise says. "Have a delicious caramel-flavoured rice cake!" She offers me the package as she and my mom burst into laughter. I guess I missed the joke, because there is nothing funny or delicious about rice cakes.

"I'm going to bed," I announce.

"So early?" Denise says. "Come on, we'll have a girls' night in."

"Every night is a girls' night in," I mutter.

"Well! We don't want that kind of attitude bringing us down, do we Annie?" Denise says.

Mom throws a protein bar at Denise. "Shush, you!" she scolds. To me, she offers her cheek. I kiss it before turning to leave. She grabs my arm and looks right at me, the way mothers do when they are trying to figure out what you're hiding. "You're sure it was fine?"

"I said it was fine."

* * *

It most certainly was *not* fine. It was the exact opposite of fine. Not that I would ever tell my mom that. I don't like to give her things to worry about. A bad audition doesn't really compare to getting cancer and losing all your hair.

In my room, I whip my bag into the corner, tear off my shoes, and throw myself on the bed, fully dressed. I punch my pillows a bit but even that doesn't make me feel better. I feel stupid and pathetic and definitely not fine. *The Wizard of Oz* is sitting on my nightstand, taunting me. I shove the book under the bed, behind a pile of empty shoeboxes that I had told my mother I threw out ages ago. Maybe this is a sign that it's time for me to move on, grow up, or at the very least, read other things.

The doorbell rings. It's Benji, I know it. I feel bad about the way home. I barely spoke a word, but it was only because I was afraid that if I opened my mouth I'd start to cry. Thank goodness for Mattie and her motormouth. If she hadn't been there the silence would have been unbearable.

I'd like to go to bed and forget the whole thing happened, like a bad dream. But I can hear my mom chatting with Benji in the kitchen, so I pull myself together and put on the happiest face I can muster. Minutes later, someone knocks tentatively on my door.

"Come in."

Benji slinks in and makes his way to my bed without saying a word. He climbs up and we lie side by side for a while until he asks, "Well, how did it go?"

"Not great," I admit. "The song was really high and my reading wasn't very good."

It doesn't feel as bad to say it out loud as I thought it would. Actually, it's kind of a relief.

"I'm sorry, Clarissa."

"It's not your fault."

"Mine was okay," Benji says. "I barely looked at the audition panel but at least I remembered the words to the song. And I didn't throw up."

"Did you show them your sketches?" I ask.

Benji shakes his head, no. "I forgot. I was just so glad the whole thing was over that I kind of bolted. But I'm glad you made me do it. You should do one thing every day that scares you."

"Who said that?"

Benji shrugs. "I don't know. It's famous. Maybe Oprah?"

"That sounds like something Oprah would say. Benji?"

"Yes?"

"Don't tell anyone what I told you, about the song and the reading and stuff."

Benji draws a cross over his heart with his finger. "Never," he swears.

Girl Talk

I'm not all that surprised that I haven't heard anything about a callback, but I feel sad about it just the same. And I am certainly not eager to talk about it when Mattie phones.

"Don't be discouraged," Mattie says. "Just because you don't get one part doesn't mean you aren't a good actress. They probably cast all high school kids anyway."

"True," I sigh.

"Plus not every role will be a singing role. You don't like to sing, right?"

I shrug. "Not really."

"Well then it wasn't meant to be."

Maybe it wasn't meant to be, but it still stinks.

"We should do something to take your mind off things," Mattie suggests. "Do you want to watch a movie?"

"Not really."

"Maybe go for a walk? We can get slushies . . ."

"Sure. Let me just call Benji."

"Oh." Mattie hesitates. "I was kind of hoping it would be just the girls. . . . Please? Just this once?"

I feel bad about not calling Benji, but we can't do everything together. Plus Mattie *was* a good friend for coming to the audition. "Okay, fine."

***

Half an hour later, I find myself sitting on a bench at the skate park watching a group of boys try to kill themselves on the ramp. At least that's what it looks like.

"Why are we here again?" I ask.

Mattie shrugs. "It's a nice place to sit," she says, but the blush in her cheeks says something else.

"Wait, are we here to watch boys?" I ask.

"No!" Mattie cries. "I just thought we could enjoy the weather."

"Enjoy the view is more like it," I say.

Mattie pretends to be offended for all of two seconds before her stern face collapses into a sheepish grin. "Okay, okay. I heard Josh talking about meeting up here and I thought maybe we could stroll by, you know, casually."

"Josh? You like Josh Simmons?"

"Why not? He's cute!"

I snort. "Maybe if you like dumb skateboarders!"

"He is not! Fine! Who do you like?"

"No one," I say, maybe a bit too quickly.

Mattie grins wickedly. "Not even Michael?"

"No way," I say. This is not exactly a lie. Michael Greenblat is the nicest boy (not including Benji) I know. He's probably the cutest too, or he would be, if he stopped wearing only sports-related clothing. Benji thinks Michael is in desperate need of a makeover, but Michael isn't the kind of boy who would let us tell him what to wear. Just the thought of Benji and Michael shopping makes me smile.

"What are you smiling about?" Mattie demands. "You do! You DO like him! I knew it. It's okay, Clarissa. You can tell me. There's nothing wrong with having a crush, especially on Michael. He's one of us."

Mattie whispers the word "us," like it's something holy. Last year Mattie, Michael, and I avenged the honour (not to mention the ribs) of Benji, who was the great Terror DiCarlo's latest (and last — he was expelled from school) victim. For a while, Michael and I were heroes, although Mattie made us promise not to tell anyone she was involved. Being involved in a prank that massive, even if it was for the good of the world, would tarnish her spotless reputation. I couldn't have pulled it off without them, and in some cosmic way we'll probably be bonded for life. Like maybe when I'm forty-five and living in an expensive villa somewhere with a full house staff, Mattie will call me up for a kidney or something and I will be obligated to give her one of mine.

Mattie was sure that Michael was in love with me, but other than a few weird gifts, nothing happened. To be honest, I was kind of relieved. After the summer, things went back to the way they were and I could think about Michael or not think about him and no one had to know anything about it. But here we are, almost a year later, and Michael did look kind of cute balancing on a skateboard.

"I guess if I had to pick someone," I finally say, "I would pick Michael —"

Mattie squeals. "I *knew* it!"

"BUT," I interrupt, pointing my finger in her face, "I'm not interested in him. Or anyone. End of story."

Mattie sighs. "*Fine*. But you would tell me if you liked someone, right?"

I think about this. Last year, there would have been no way I would tell her anything private. But, surprisingly, Mattie Cohen was quickly becoming one of my best friends. Second to Benji, of course. It turns out she's pretty funny, and you never run out of things to talk about when you're with Mattie.

"Right."

Mattie smiles and links her arm through mine. It's kind of weird and kind of nice at the same time. I'm glad the boys are too interested in their skateboards to notice. "Good!" Mattie gushes. "Trust is everything in friendship."

***

I return home to find half of my mom's running group loitering in our kitchen. They're training for the Run for the Cure marathon in October. No one was more surprised than me when Mom decided she was going to create a team, but when Denise agreed to join I think I walked around with my jaw hanging open for an entire day. Denise wheezes after sprinting from the car to the house, how was she going to handle a marathon?

"You don't have to run the whole thing, lots of people walk it," Denise explained. "It's the thought that counts. Well, that and the sponsors. Besides, I could use a little tuning up." Denise attempted to flex her arm and ended up flapping the skin where the triceps should be. Disgusting.

Mom and Denise are perfectly positioned to get lots of donations. Mom set up a stand with flyers and information on how to donate right at the front desk when you walk into the Hair Emporium. All of my mom's clients already knew about her having cancer and they just love her to pieces, so of course everyone can find a little something to donate. Denise spends most of her time sweet-talking people into buying lipstick, so it's not hard for her to talk up her best friend's battle with cancer and how they're doing something to give back.

"Hey there, Minipop!"

I didn't think it was possible to meet someone more annoying than Denise. I was wrong. I just hadn't met Janine yet. After training, Janine and Denise come over for tea and protein bars, taking over the kitchen with their gossiping and casual stretching. The whole room smells like Lycra. In order to get to the cereal, I have to duck under Janine's leg, propped up on the counter for a hamstring stretch.

I mumble a reply and rummage in the fridge for whatever milk substitute my mother is subjecting us to this week. Looks like soy. Oh well, soy milk is better than goat's milk.

"Your mom tells us you're going to be a big star," Janine chirps.

"Well I don't know," I demur. "I haven't got in yet."

"What, are you crazy?" Denise cries. "You're the biggest drama queen I know! Of course you'll get in!"

The ladies titter at Denise's bad joke.

"We'll be able to say we knew you when," Mom says with a smile. "You and Benji both."

"Who's Benji?" Janine asks. "Your boyfriend?"

I roll my eyes. "No, he's just a friend." After seven years of people assuming Benji is my boyfriend it doesn't bother me anymore.

"Oh sure, for now," Janine says, leaning in and giving me a wink. "But you'd like him to be more, right?"

"I wouldn't hold my breath if I were you, Clarissa," Denise says. "Falling in love with Benji is a recipe for disaster. Remember George Blakely?" She looks at Janine and Mom and all three nod and make sad noises.

"I am not in love with Benji. I am not in love with anyone, thank you very much."

"Good for you, Minipop. Love is more trouble than it's worth. Look at my husband, Gary. A more clueless man you've never met. Spends half his time at work, half his time with the boys doing god-knows what. I'd probably be better off with a mop. But I love the guy, so here we are."

Poor Gary. I'd make myself scarce if Janine was my wife, too.

"Don't scare the poor girl, Janine!" Denise scolds. "Some men are worth the trouble. Like Doug . . . wouldn't you agree, Annie?" Both women look slyly at my mother, who has been suspiciously quiet this whole time.

Mom smiles her blithe, Mona Lisa smile. "He is what they call a good egg."

Denise snorts. "A good egg? He's an omelette!"

Janine shakes her head. "Honey, that man is a whole chicken!" She high-fives Denise and the two of them howl with laughter.

If you ask me, there are two too many people in the kitchen. Mom looks at me and winks.

"Annie, can you give me a little trim?" Janine asks.

"Sure, let me get settled." Mom heads down to the Hair Emporium and Denise helps herself to a third protein bar.

"Well if you're going to get your hair done, I might as well stick around and chat for a bit," she says.

Janine smiles at me. "What do you say, Minipop? Wanna join the girls for some girl talk?"

I've spent a lot of time with girls today. Besides, I can think of a million things I'd rather do than talk about menopause or dating after forty with Denise and Janine. Luckily, the perfect excuse lives right next door.

"No, thanks. I told Benji I'd stop by." And before anyone can make another egg joke, I'm gone.

Gone

"What in God's name is the matter?"

I step back, surprised to see Benji's father on the other side of the door. He is rumpled and grumpy looking with pillow creases on his rather stubbly cheek. Normally he'd be at work at this time. He must be on nights this week, which means I've interrupted his sleep. Waking Mr. Denton is kind of like waking a bear; a big, hockey-playing bear. Not a good idea if you can help it. There's a reason his old hockey buddies still call him the Dentonator; years after his days as a goon on the local Junior A team, he still looks like he could knock you right into the Arctic Circle with one shoulder.

"Oh, sorry Mr. D. I was looking for Benji."

"He's not here. He had to go to the theatre for something or other."

"The theatre?"

The Dentonator grunts. "That's what he said. I figured you were with him. Didn't you know? Well?"

I'm so caught off guard it takes me a moment to realize that the Dentonator is staring at me, waiting for me to say something. "I'm not sure, Mr. D. He never mentioned anything about the theatre to me."

The Dentonator frowns. "Huh? I thought you two were attached at the brain."

It is weird. Benji never does anything without telling me about it. Why would he go to the theatre without me? Then again, I went to the park with Mattie without inviting him. A pang of guilt stabs me in the gut. What if he called and found out I was with Mattie? What if he saw us leave the house? Maybe this was karma.

"Did he say when he'd be back?" I ask.

"Nope, but I'll tell him you were here." And with that the Dentonator shuts the door, probably lumbering back to his room to hibernate.

***

I have to do something to keep my mind off Benji's mysterious trip to the theatre. Television didn't work. Homework certainly didn't work. How am I supposed to focus on exponents when my best friend is hiding something from me? I couldn't even paint my toenails. Where is Benji? What is taking him so long? I positioned myself in the dining room so I can see the Dentons' side door — the only door they ever use. When Benji comes home, I'll be the first to know.

Four o'clock slips by, then four-thirty, and somehow it's five. I can hear Mom chatting away to a client, laughter travelling up the air vents from the basement to the dining room. It's a nice sound. She's almost back to a full-time schedule. At first she was worried that her customers would find a new stylist. She underestimates the power of a good head massage. That plus the vanilla-scented candles.

Unable to stand it a second longer, I shove my arms into my jacket, run down the basement stairs, and stick my head into the Hair Emporium.

29

"Mom? I'm going to the theatre."

Mom looks over from blowdrying Mrs. Seto's hair. "It's almost dinner," she says.

"I won't be long," I promise.

Mrs. Seto sits up, flipping her freshly cut hair back over her shoulders. "Clarissa, I heard you auditioned for the musical."

I shoot Mom a look. I know she's a hair stylist and every-thing, but does everyone have to know our business?

"Yes," I say slowly. "But I don't think it went very well."

"That's too bad," says Mrs. Seto. "I'm stage-managing and if you want to get involved we always need people back-stage, or making props and costumes."

Costumes! Of course! Benji probably went to the theatre to submit his costume designs. It's so obvious I feel stupid for not figuring it out before. I'm so relieved and grateful to Mrs. Seto I tell her that I would think about joining her crew. Unlikely. I am meant to be *on* stage, not behind it.

***

I go to the theatre anyway, to walk Benji home. I'm so proud of him. Benji is a really great artist. He draws all sorts of things, from comics to costume designs to goofy cards. If he wasn't so darn shy maybe he'd get more recognition. I don't understand him sometimes. You can bet if I could draw even half as well as he can, I'd be showing the whole world. It must be nice to be that good at something. I was kind of hoping that acting would be my thing, but that didn't seem to be working out as well as I'd hoped. If only I could sing. I bet if my mother had put me in singing lessons when I was little I'd be just as good as Charity Smith-Jones. Maybe I would be the one with the Tim Hortons commercial.

At the theatre, the parking lot is surprisingly full. People are hanging around the front steps in groups of twos and threes, chatting. I weave through them to the big double doors and head inside. In the lobby, a desk is sitting in front of the auditorium doors, just like it was at the auditions. The sign that reads SHHH! AUDITIONS IN PROCESS is still taped to the front from yesterday. I can hear muffled voices from inside the auditorium, but there is no one in the lobby.

I wonder if they've started rehearsals already. That seems pretty soon after auditions to me, but what do I know about theatre? I can't even get a part in a stupid community show. I can feel a bad mood coming on like a storm in August, but I try to shake it off. If I could just find Benji we could leave and I could go back to having a good day. Being at the theatre reminds me of how awful my audition was. This must be what criminals feel when they return to the scene of a crime.

The corkboard beside the drinking fountain is covered in posters for music lessons and art clubs. So what if I'm not a good actress? Maybe I could take up an instrument. It would be pretty cool to play the fiddle. I think about tearing off one of the strips with a phone number for a music teacher named Miss Bell. That can't be a coincidence. Then I see the schedule. Across the top it reads WIZARD OF OZ CALLBACKS. Underneath is a list of time slots with names pencilled in beside them. Halfway down the page, next to the slot labelled 3 to 5 pm, is Benjamin Denton.

Lies

I'm still staring at the callback schedule when the doors swing open and people pour out of the auditorium. I jump away from the notice board, ripping off one of Miss Bell's phone numbers. I study it intently, like maybe I'm trying to memorize the number by heart. Someone with untied shoelaces stops a few steps away from me. I'd recognize those shoes anywhere. Benji is the only person I know who can wear shoes without tying them up and not trip all over his own feet.

"Clarissa?" he says. "What are you doing here?"

Do I detect a note of suspicion? I look up. Benji is flushed.

"What are *you* doing here?" I repeat.

Benji looks helplessly at the schedule. He doesn't need to say anything. We both know I've seen it.

"Oh, right, your callback."

"I was going to tell you . . ." Benji starts weakly, but I cut him off.

"When?" I demand.

Benji shrugs. He looks miserable. I feel bad. If I was Benji, would I want to tell me about the callback? Probably not. He's always thinking about how other people feel. Time to change tactics.

"Well? How did it go?"

Benji brightens a little but he still looks wary. "Actually, I think it went really well." He breaks into a smile. "Really, really well."

My heart lurches with jealousy. "Really? That's great." My voice sounds strained, but Benji doesn't seem to notice.

"So, what are you doing here?" Benji asks again.

"I thought you came by to drop off your sketches. I came to pick you up."

Benji smiles widely. "Thanks."

Another group of people swings through the auditorium doors, including Charity Smith-Jones. She spots us and waves. "Hey, Benjamin. I really liked what you did in there. Good stuff!"

Benji blushes. "Thanks, Charity. You were really great. I hope you get the part."

Charity looks over her shoulder at her friends, who are all much older. She leans in and whispers, "Don't tell those I guys I said this, but I hope you do, too." Then she winks and jogs off to join the other kids who are now breaking into what I can only imagine is the audition dance.

The second we're out of earshot I turn around and give Benji the eye. "Hey, *Benjamin?* Thanks, *Charity?* You're on a first-name basis with her now?"

"She's really nice," Benji claims. "And she's a really good singer." He pauses before adding, "She's probably going to get Dorothy. Sorry."

"It's not your fault," I sigh, even though, in my opinion, that is the kind of information he could have kept to himself. Reluctantly I ask, "So, tell me what happened."

It turns out he got a callback for the Cowardly Lion. He had to learn a bit of a song and part of a dance routine.

Then they made him read lines with Charity and another girl I've never heard of before.

"Wow, Benji. That's great."

"I'm sorry I didn't tell you before, Clarissa. I wanted to, but then Mattie said —"

I stop walking.

"Wait — *Mattie* said? Mattie knew about this?"

"I had to tell someone," he says plaintively, "and I knew you were upset about your audition so I called Mattie and asked her what I should do."

So many light bulbs are going off inside my head it must be like Christmas in there. Mattie was the one who said not to call Benji. Mattie was the one who wanted to leave the house and hang out at the park, which is in the opposite direction of the theatre. It was all a plot to keep me in the dark.

"Clarissa, please don't be mad. You know you would've been upset! I saw your face in there, you were upset! I just didn't want to hurt your feelings . . ." Benji trails off.

"I know," I grumble.

"I hate it when you're mad," Benji finishes.

"I'm not mad," I protest.

Which is true. I'm not mad. At him.

***

For the rest of the walk home, I try to convince Benji that I'm not mad and pretend that everything is normal between us. It is the best performance of my life. If only the audition panel could see me now.

The second I get home I fly in the door and run for the phone.

"Hey there, missy, dinner is in two minutes —"

"One sec, Mom!"

I dodge past her and start dialling Mattie's number without even taking my coat or shoes off.

Mattie answers on the second ring. "Hello, Cohen residence."

"It's Clarissa."

"Hi, Clarissa! What's up?"

"You told me you wanted to spend time just us girls," I say.

"I don't understand . . ."

"This afternoon! At the park! You said you wanted to hang out just us girls!"

I'm yelling now. Mom comes into the living room, frowning. "Clarissa, what on earth —"

"You lied to me! You knew Benji had that callback and you didn't want me to know so you lied to me! And you got Benji to lie to me!"

"No, I didn't —" Mattie protests.

"Yes, you did!"

"Benji was worried you'd be upset and listen to you, you ARE upset! You would have ruined his callback!"

I'm so offended I don't even know what to say. Mattie keeps going. "He needed your support but you would have freaked out, so I told him to wait. It was best for you and Benji! If you would just calm down and let me explain it to you, I'm sure you'd agree."

"Don't tell me what's best for me!" I shout. "You barely know me! And you don't know Benji like I do! I would never upset him, I'm happy for him. The only person I'm mad at is you."

"Clarissa, I can explain," Mattie whimpers.

"What did you say this afternoon? Trust is everything? Well how am I supposed to trust you now?"

There. That shut her up. I slam the phone down and take a deep breath. My throat hurts from screaming. Mom is staring at me.

"Don't ask," I warn her.

"All that yelling has given me indigestion. I think I have the right to know why my dinner has been ruined."

"Maybe you shouldn't have been eavesdropping," I say.

Mom crosses her arms and stares me down. Her short hair makes her look even tougher when she's mad. "That's enough, Clarissa. I've heard quite enough from you just now. I don't need any of that smart mouth."

I jam my teeth together and will myself to be quiet. If I don't, I'll just make it worse. Why does everything have to go wrong at once? Isn't it enough that Benji got a callback and I didn't? Why did he have to tell Mattie and not me? Why did they have to come up with a plan to not tell me? And now Mom is mad. I wish I could fast-forward to my twenty-fifth birthday. Or at least next year.

Hard

The phone rings when I'm in the bathtub, trying to calm down. Mom says the best place to cool down is in a hot tub. I don't understand how or why it works, but it does. I'm scrubbing last week's nail polish from my toes when Mom taps on the door.

"Phone," she calls.

"I'm busy," I mutter.

"I can't hear you," she replies.

"I'm busy!" I shout.

"It's Benji."

I drag myself out of the bath, wrap myself in my robe, open the door, and grab the phone from my mother. "I was in the bath."

"Sorry. I can call you back."

"No, no, I'm out now. So?"

"So . . . I heard."

My heart beats a little faster. "And?"

"I got in; I'm going to be the Cowardly Lion."

Not even the splittest of seconds passes before I launch into the congratulations I'd planned in the bathtub, just in case. "Benji, that's amazing!"

"I still can't believe it. You should have seen my dad. He didn't know what to say."

The image of the Dentonator trying to grapple with the idea of his son singing and dancing onstage makes me giggle and I feel a little less torn.

"Are you okay?" Benji asks.

"Of course I'm okay," I lie. "I'm better than okay, I'm so happy for you. They couldn't ask for a better lion." Most of this is true, but it doesn't stop my heart from aching.

"Okay, good." Benji's relief flows across the telephone line. "I wish you were going to be in it," he adds.

"Me too," I admit.

"It's going to be weird not having you there."

"You'll probably meet all these new, super-cool people and forget all about me," I say lightly, hoping against hope that it won't turn out to be true.

"Clarissa, you are the most unforgettable person I know, except for maybe Denise."

"Denise doesn't count. How can I compete with that honking laugh?"

"She should really be exempt."

"She should."

There is a pause in the conversation that I can't seem to find the words to fill. My heart feels sore in a million places. But as sad as I am about not getting the role of my dreams, I have to find a way to lock it all up and just be happy for Benji. It shouldn't be so difficult, he's my best friend, for crying out loud. Part of me wants him to do well, but a bigger part of me wishes that I could be there to do well beside him.

"Well, goodnight. And congratulations again, Benji."

"Thanks, Clarissa. I'm glad you're okay with everything, because if you wanted me to . . . well . . . I would quit."

"Absolutely not," I say. "Don't be stupid."

"It's just a play, you're my best friend."

38

"It is *not* just a play; it's *The Wizard of Oz*! It's up to you to do it justice! And you are *my* best friend, and I won't let you quit just because I wasn't good enough to get in."

"Charity says casting is not about being good, it's about being right for the part."

Charity says? He just met her, and already he's quoting her? I try not to let on that this bothers me. Instead I say as brightly as possible, "Well, I guess she would know!"

"She's really nice. I think you'd like her."

"I'm sure I would," I say quickly. "Goodnight."

"'night."

I hang up the phone and change into an old t-shirt and gym shorts, ready for bed, even though it's barely eight o'clock. I think about watching TV or reading or doing something to make me feel less miserable, but all I want to do is lie on the bed and stew in my bad mood.

"I gather he got in." Mom appears in the doorway in her silent ninja-mom way, holding a tall, frothy glass of what can only be . . .

"Creamsicle float?" I ask.

Mom nods. "I figured you could use a pick-me-up."

I nod wordlessly, slip off the bed, and take the glass from her hand. It feels cold and smooth and just holding it lifts my spirits a little. Mom makes the best ice cream floats in the world. She uses only premium vanilla ice cream and no-name orange pop. You would think that the more expensive stuff would taste better, but we have done the research and it turns out the cheap-o drugstore brand is the best.

"That was good of you, on the phone," Mom says. "I know it couldn't have been easy."

"I guess." I shrug, refusing to look her in the eye. If I do, she'll look at me in that way that melts all the hard things inside of me and I'll turn into a soggy, blubbering cry-baby.

Mom puts an arm around my shoulder and guides me back to the bed. We sit, me drinking my float, and Mom drawing circles across my shoulder blades with her fingernails. It feels nice. When I was little, she used to write words with her finger and I would try and guess what they were.

I can't remember the last time she sat on the bed with me and scratched my back. Ever since her diagnosis, I do my best to appear happy and worry-free, even on really bad days. Maybe it's superstitious, but I believe in that saying about making yourself sick with worry. My mom already *is* sick, and I don't want to make it worse by giving her something else to worry about. But this time, try as I might, I can't stop them from coming — big, heaving sobs. I try to fight them off, but I'm so cozy and my mom is right there.

"It's just —" I start, but the words get caught in a full-body sob.

"Yes?" Mom encourages.

"I'm the one who always wanted to act."

"I know."

"And I'm not mad at him, how can you possibly be mad at Benji, but —" I take a deep breath, trying to steady my voice, "why couldn't we both get in?" Hot tears run down my cheeks. There is nothing I can do to stop them. I am officially crying.

Mom lets me go for a while, rubbing my back and shoulders. When I've calmed myself down, she continues, "I'm sorry you didn't get in, Clarissa. It took a lot of guts to get up and audition for something like that. You should be so proud of yourself. I know I am proud of you. And next time it will be that much easier."

40

"I don't know if there will be a next time," I mumble.

"There will be. If you really want to be an actress you have to get back out there and try again. You have to get used to rejection."

I stare into my empty glass so I don't have to answer.

"Benji needs a break like this," Mom continues, "and I'm not saying that you don't deserve it, either, but we both know you are made of stronger stuff. You feel awful now, but you will bounce back. And you're going to have to hear all about rehearsals and costumes and pretend it doesn't hurt."

"I know," I sigh.

"What Benji needs most is your support."

Mom takes my chin in her hand and smiles at me like I am something miraculous and not some dripping, red-eyed mess. "Look at you," she sighs, "practically all grown up, only a few months away from grade nine. You know, high school is a whole different ball game. You and Benji won't always do the same things, but that doesn't mean you can't still be best friends."

"I know that."

"Good. Now, do you feel better, or should I make another float?"

In our post-diagnosis world of celery and soy milk, a real ice cream float is a rare thing.

"I think one more will make me feel a whole lot better."

Mom laughs. "I figured. Well, get up. The least you can do is come keep me company while I work my magic."

Miss

Benji has rehearsal Tuesdays and Thursdays after school, Saturday mornings, and every other Sunday afternoon. When he's not at rehearsal it seems like he's either catching up on his homework or practising his lines. Considering we used to spend almost every waking moment together, it's been weird adjusting to his new schedule.

A secret part of me is relieved. I don't think I could handle hearing about how much fun he's having in the show I should have been in. I thought the disappointment would fade but it's still there, niggling away like a sad song I just can't get out of my head. Consequently, I've been spending more and more time with Mattie. After receiving many weepy phone calls and I'm Sorry notes written in sparkly pen, I decided to forgive her for the Don't Tell Clarissa About Benji's Callback fiasco. I know why she did it, and I can't really blame her. But even though Mattie can be lots of fun, she doesn't exactly fill the Benji-shaped hole in my life.

On Thursdays I go home with Mattie and stay for dinner, which works out perfectly because Mom trains at the gym Thursday evening. Mattie's mom is always waiting for us when we walk in the door. She kisses Mattie on both cheeks and gives me a hug before asking, "What would you girls like for a snack?"

"Oh I'm fine, Cheryl," I tell her. "I have my Mr. Noodles left over from lunch."

Cheryl Cohen frowns. "Oh, Clarissa, let me cut you an apple. We don't eat dehydrated food around here."

"It's bad for you," Mattie adds.

I rip the silver packet and dump the powdery flavour and pieces of dried carrot and onion and beef onto my noodles. "Astronauts eat dehydrated food," I point out.

"They're in space," Mattie says patiently, like she's talking to an idiot instead of someone who got a higher mark on her last science test that she did. "They don't have any choice."

I tip the kettle and pour steaming hot water to the line etched into the cup. "Well, I *do* have a choice and if it's good enough for an astronaut, then it's good enough for me."

Mattie and her mother exchange disgusted glances but have nothing more to say. How can you argue with science?

Most of the time, I drink my milk (there is no pop at the Cohen house), and listen. It's weird watching another mom and daughter together, but I definitely don't miss Denise's third-wheel commentary. At first I worried that maybe *I* was the third wheel, but I got over that pretty quickly. Mattie and her mom just love having people over, almost as much as they love talking. Mattie tells her mom absolutely everything that happens in school, including who said what, and what so and so was wearing. Sometimes they even try to figure out the motives behind people's behaviour.

"I'm not surprised that Amanda and Min have been spending so much time together," Cheryl says. "Amanda has always needed someone to follow and Min is a bit of a queen bee."

Eventually Mattie runs out of things to report and Cheryl says, "Well I'll let you two girls get down to your homework," as if she's been keeping us from the joy of long division. "But first, why don't you pick out a CD that we can listen to while I make dinner?"

By CD she means one of her cheesy compilation albums. Cheryl Cohen has every single "Women & Songs" CD, and apparently nothing else. There must be about ten of them. Mattie takes forever to choose, scanning the song list and eventually narrowing the selection down to two and allowing me to make the final decision. I don't see what the big deal is. "Women & Songs 1" sounds exactly like "Women & Songs 10." Normally I would do my homework in front of the TV, but Mattie only watches one hour of TV a day on weekdays. I never thought I would miss all those corny re-runs that Benji makes us watch, but even *Full House* is better than "Women & Songs."

***

When I get home, Denise is lounging in a chair, my mother wrapping thick sections of her rusty-coloured hair around a large-barrelled curling iron.

"What's going on?" I ask.

"Denise has a big date, so I'm giving her the Cosmo blow-out."

It's a good thing I'm not chewing any gum, because I would have spit it right into Denise's hard-earned curls in shock.

"A date?" I repeat. "With who?"

It must be a big date because the Cosmo blow-out — so named because it is the hairstyle they give to every single actress or model who appears on the front of *Cosmo* magazine — is a lot of work, involving hot rollers, two different curling irons, and a lot of hairspray.

Denise whacks me lightly on the arm. I admit my tone may have been a tad suspicious. "Dennis."

It takes me a moment to respond. "Dennis?" I say carefully.

Mom frowns. "Yes, Dennis."

"Denise is going on a date with a man named Dennis?"

Mom's lip twitches as it dawns on her just how similar the names Dennis and Denise are. Maybe she hadn't heard them spoken aloud together. "Yes," she repeats evenly, in a masterful attempt to hide any amusement. "Denise is going on a date with a man named Dennis."

I glance at Denise to see if the light bulb had gone off in her head, but she is filing away, squaring off her nails in preparation for her date. With Dennis.

"I met him in line at the grocery store, can you believe it? I guess Oprah was right. You never know when you're going to meet that certain someone," Denise says.

"A certain someone named Dennis. Who you, Denise, are going out on a date with."

Mom shoots me a look but Denise doesn't seem to pick up on it. "For Pete's sake, Clarissa," she asks, "what's gotten into you? What's so hard to believe?"

"Nothing, it's just that —"

"You just can't imagine someone asking me out? Is that it?"

Well, yes, but that wasn't the point.

I sigh. When you have to explain the joke it really wasn't all that funny. I needed an appreciative audience. I need Benji. Why does he have to be at stupid rehearsal all the time?

Doug

"Is that a man?"

Benji and I stop dead in our tracks and listen. Downstairs in the Hair Emporium, Mom is talking to someone who does, in fact, sound like a man. Mom only has three male clients: Denise's brother-in-law Richard, a nervous man who rarely speaks if he can help it; old Mr. Lawford, who looks like he's pushing one hundred years old; and Benji, of course. None of them sounds like the mystery man. All I can hear is rumbling interrupted by a throaty laugh. What could he possibly be laughing at? My mother is not that funny. Beautiful, yes, but not funny.

"Come on," I tell Benji. We drop our backpacks and head down the stairs.

"Mom? I'm home."

"Oh, Clarissa, come on in. I want you to meet Doug."

Doug. The good egg. My mother's trainer.

Seated in my mother's red leather recliner, the cape tied around his neck and barely reaching his thighs, Doug looks like a giant. His legs seem to go on forever, stretched out in front of him and ending in big, yellow workboots with the laces untied. They are suspiciously clean, as if no actual work is done while wearing those boots.

Doug's hair is damp and falls in longish waves on either

side of his part, no doubt discovered by my mother and her little red comb. He keeps slicking it back, which causes my mom to slap his wrist with her comb, which makes him laugh, and then she laughs. Is my mother flirting?

Doug stands to shake my hand and my suspicions are confirmed; he is officially the tallest man I have ever seen in real life. "Hey there, Clarissa, nice to finally meet you. And let me guess, you must be Benji? The star?"

I only bristle a little as Benji blushes and says, "I'm not the star, I'm just the Lion."

"And what trouble did you two get up to today?" Doug asks, easing himself back onto the recliner.

"Math, English, Geography, the usual," I say evenly.

Doug laughs. "Touché."

"Doug is finally letting me give him a much-needed trim," Mom says, rubbing the ends of Doug's hair between her fingers and making her "yuck, split ends" face.

Doug shrugs. "She wore me down. Plus I've been meaning to check out the Hair Emporium. See what all the fuss is about."

"The fuss!" Mom exclaims. "Well, I hope it lives up to your high standards. When is the last time you had your hair cut, anyway? Prom?"

Doug grins. "Nah, I think it was my sweet sixteen."

Mom smiles wickedly. "Well, fifty years is long enough, don't you think?"

Doug laughs long and hard, slapping his thigh. Mom looks very pleased with herself.

"Promise me you won't buzz it all off," Doug says. "My hair is my trademark. It's the source of all my powers."

My breath catches in my throat. How stupid can you be, making hair jokes in front of a person who just recently lost her hair? It doesn't seem to resonate with Mom, who is still grinning away, turning Doug's head this way and that, visualizing the cut in the mirror.

"Yes, I'm sure if we cut it all off, the female membership at the gym would drop off significantly," she says dryly.

Benji's eyes almost fall right out of his skull. We exchange horrified glances. My mother is most definitely flirting. Doug laughs again but this time, if I'm not mistaken, his face turns a little pink.

"Okay, I've got it," Mom says. "Do you trust me?"

"Annie, there isn't another stylist on the entire planet I'd trust more."

I have to work hard not to roll my eyes. Doug and Mom are grinning at each other in the mirror. Her hands are resting on his shoulders and she's leaning forward so they are practically cheek to cheek. Suddenly the salon feels too small for four people.

"Well, it was nice to meet you, Doug. We've got some homework to do, so . . ." I gesture toward the door and start backing out.

Mom doesn't even look over, but waves in our direction. "Bye kids, there are some donuts in the kitchen if you're hungry."

"Donuts?" I repeat. I can't believe it; they were on the list of foods that Doug himself had outlawed at the beginning of my mom's marathon training.

"Doug brought them. He knows how much I've been missing my Boston creams."

"Consider it part of your tip," Doug jokes.

Benji and I head upstairs, their laughter following us all the way into the kitchen. Sure enough, there's a paper bag with grease stains on the bottom sitting on the counter.

I grab the bag of donuts and step back into my shoes. "Come on," I say to Benji. "We're going to your place."

* * *

I should have known something was up when I started to hear Mom laughing into the phone after dinner. I knew it couldn't be Denise, because Mom always finds things to do while she's on the phone with her: paint her toenails, pluck her eyebrows, or flip through a magazine. But this person — whoever it was — on the other side of the line had captured her full attention. Plus she told stories that I knew Denise had already heard. Some of them were even about Denise. I listened carefully for any mention of my name, but if she did talk about me, it was in a hushed tone that couldn't be heard on the other side of the wall that separated our bedrooms.

Now it all made perfect sense.

Once we're out of earshot, in Benji's den with the TV on and the donuts between us, I can say what I'm really thinking. "Well. Can you believe that — flirting? At their age?"

"Sure," Benji says. "Your mom's beautiful and Doug's handsome, so yeah. I can believe it."

"You think he's handsome?"

Benji looks surprised. "You don't?"

"I don't know, his hair is kind of long."

"Maybe for you, but not for women of a certain age," Benji points out, adding, "I think it's nice that your mom has a crush."

"Ugh, stop!" I cry, covering my ears. "It sounds so wrong! Mothers do not get crushes!"

Benji grins wickedly. "Your mom totally has a crush," he says, just to torture me.

49

I shudder at the thought. "There was just so much giggling. Grown women shouldn't giggle."

Benji laughs and takes a dainty bite out of a donut.

"What are you doing?" I ask. "Just shove the whole thing in."

"I can't," Benji says, tearing the donut in half and putting part of it back in the bag. "I shouldn't be eating donuts at all. I have to fit into my Lion costume. It's already a little tight."

I roll my eyes. "What is the world coming to? My mom is flirting and you're on a diet."

Benji's eyes shine. "Wait till Mattie finds out. I can almost hear her squealing now."

***

Benji was right, of course. Mattie can't get enough of the idea of my mom and Doug the trainer.

"Don't you think it's romantic?" she insists. "A young, single mother is tragically struck with cancer. She beats it — against all odds — and decides to give back to the medical community by participating in a fundraising marathon. And that's when she meets the man of her dreams, a hot trainer who sees both her inner and outer beauty!"

"You make it sound like a movie," I complain. I don't point out that my mom hasn't exactly beat the odds, not yet.

"I'd go see that movie," Benji says.

"Me, too!" Mattie gushes. "Except it's better than a movie, it's real life!"

"Sandra Bullock could play your mom," Benji says.

Mattie frowns. "No, her colouring isn't right." Benji and Mattie brainstorm actresses to play the role of my mother.

"What about me?" I ask.

"You would play yourself, obviously," Mattie declares.

Hmm. This movie idea isn't sounding so bad after all. Can you still be nominated for an Oscar for playing yourself in a movie?

"This is so exciting, when is the last time your mother had a boyfriend?" Mattie asks.

I don't even have to think about it. "Never."

Mattie can't believe it. "Never? Not even once?"

"Not even once," I confirm.

For ten blissful seconds, Mattie is speechless, trying to fathom how my mother has remained single all these years. My whole life, it's always been me and Mom and, regrettably, Denise. Men had never entered the picture before. This was unfamiliar territory and I wasn't sure I liked it. Why now, after all these years?

"That is unbelievable!" Mattie says. "Your mom is so beautiful! And nice! And smart! There must be tons of men who would want to date her. I wonder what happened."

I shrug. "Maybe she wasn't interested in anyone."

"Impossible. Everyone has crushes." Mattie looks right at me before adding, "Well, *almost* everyone."

"I used to wish she'd marry my dad," Benji admits.

Mattie smiles kindly at him but even she knows a lost cause when she sees one. Changing the topic, she concludes, "Well, Doug must be an amazing person. After all these years, he's teaching her how to feel again."

I roll my eyes. "My mom *feels* things, she just isn't gushy like some people."

Mattie looks pointedly at me. "I guess it runs in the family." I give her a grade-A glare. Benji looks confused.

"Did I miss something?" he asks.

Mattie sighs. "No," she says. "Clarissa's the one who doesn't get it."

Help

A perfect Friday night consists of me, Benji, pizza, and a movie. Sometimes we pick out something new, but usually we just channel surf until we find something we like.

If there isn't anything good on, we pick the worst movie we can find, put the sound on mute, and make up our own dialogue. Tonight is one of those nights. It's Benji's turn to pick, and he chooses some movie of the week on the Women's Network. I don't know for sure, but it appears to be about a scandalous love affair in a Mennonite community. I have decided to adopt a Spanish accent for the voice of the female lead, who looks vaguely Hispanic and not Mennonite at all.

"Oh, John Jacob Jingleheimer Schmidt, I love how your muscles ripple under that shapeless tunic," I gush.

Benji giggles and then replies in his best cowboy voice, "Senorita Bellissima, you know I cannot love you. I already have a wife and twenty-five children. But oh, how you haunt my dreams."

"I shall haunt you forever, until you agree to leave this place and marry me," I say passionately, being sure to roll my R's.

"Where would we go?"

"Perhaps we could go to America, the promised land."

Benji drops his deep-voiced tough-guy act. "Wait, aren't we already in the States?"

I throw a cushion at him. "Do you have to be so literal all the time? Use your imagination! I would think you of all people would appreciate an acting exercise like this."

Benji shrugs and helps himself to another piece of pizza. The silence is stretching on a little too long. Something is up.

"What's wrong?" I ask. "Are you offended?"

"No," Benji says slowly. "It's just . . . can I ask you a question?"

"Shoot."

"Do you swear to answer honestly, even if it means hurting my feelings?"

"I'm always honest," I protest, but seeing the look on Benji's face I add, "with you, anyway."

"Do you think I make a good Lion?"

Great. *Wizard of Oz* talk. I smile and try to brush it off so we can move on to something else. "What? Of course you do! You got a lead in a musical, didn't you?"

Benji chews on his pizza thoughtfully. "I know, but I was thinking . . . please don't laugh when I tell you this . . ."

"I won't," I promise.

"Well, the other day at rehearsal, I was doing the scene where Dorothy first meets the Cowardly Lion. Everyone laughed — which is good, it's supposed to be funny — but then I started to wonder, what if they were laughing *at* me?"

"What do you mean?"

"I mean, I know I'm not the best singer in the world, and I've never acted before, and look at me, there is nothing lion-like about me."

This is true. Physically Benji looks more like the Scarecrow than a lion.

53

"So what if the only reason they cast me is because it's funny that a skinny kid like me is playing the Lion? You know, like when they cast that wrestler as the tooth fairy?"

"You saw that movie?" I scoff.

"No, but you know the one I mean."

I did. It was the kind of movie I would only see if I had to choose between it and poking my own eyes out.

"I think you're overreacting," I say, but Benji still looks miserable. I hate seeing him like this; it reminds me of those sad-eyed puppies that stare out at you from the window of the pet store in the mall. Plus I really don't like talking about the play. I know a better person would have put it behind her by now, but my insides still clench up when I think about how Charity Smith-Jones, not Clarissa Louise Delaney, will be playing Dorothy.

"Would you help me? I mean, would it be weird if you practised with me?" Benji asks.

I draw on all my acting skills to keep my face composed. "Me?"

"No one knows *The Wizard of Oz* like you do, and I know you'll be honest with me."

"I don't know," I protest.

Benji droops a little bit and I remind myself that this is not about me, it's about Benji. To my surprise and mild horror, I find myself thinking about what Mattie would do in this situation. I hate to admit it, but she is a much better person than I am. Mattie would definitely help out. Reading those lines with him will be hard, but Benji is worth it.

"Okay, but just for a little while."

Benji brightens. "Really?"

"Really."

Benji rummages in his backpack until he finds his copy

of the script. He flips to the right page and hands it to me. His lines are highlighted in pink. "Here, you read everything that isn't marked."

And so Benji and I read through the scene. It hurts to read Dorothy's lines and know that I am not going to be the one saying them on stage. But for Benji's sake, I give it my best. After all, an actor needs something to play off.

When we finish, Benji looks at me expectantly. "Well?"

I can't know the exact reasons why the director cast him. Yes, he is a little on the small side for a lion and, yes, his voice is a little warbly at times. But he is sweet and he is earnest and isn't that what the Cowardly Lion is all about? Maybe I'm not good enough to be in the show, but Benji is. Not that I would ever admit that first part out loud.

"Benji, you are going to be great. You're funny in all the right ways."

Benji takes a deep breath and I can almost see the weight lifting off his shoulders and vanishing into thin air. "This is a lot harder than I thought it was going to be," he admits.

Tell me about it.

"Benji, you are going to be great."

He smiles weakly. "Thanks. I knew you'd tell me the truth."

I may not be a good enough actress to get into a community production of *The Wizard of Oz*, but I am a great cheerleader.

Time

It's rare to get a moment alone with Mom these days. There are always people hanging around: her clients, Denise, the running team, and now Doug and his dog.

Mom has stepped up her training and it seems like Doug is over every other day, bringing protein shakes or articles or just dropping by to say hello. He may have won my mother over, but I refuse to be charmed. He must have picked up on this, because Doug has started bringing over his dog, Suzy. If he thinks I am the kind of person who can be won over by a puppy, then he is sadly mistaken. I am not that girl. I am not Mattie Cohen, who cries at TV commercials about the animal shelter and stops to pet every dog we pass on the street. I'm not even sure I like dogs. I know I don't like the way they smell, or that you have to walk behind them with a bag to pick up their poop. If you ask me, dogs are more trouble than they're worth. So when Doug comes over with Suzy, who looks more like a mop than a dog, I am not impressed.

Sometimes I wish Mom would send everyone away and we could just hang out together. We wouldn't have to do anything special, maybe just watch a movie and do our nails. I can't bring myself to ask about it, because if she asks why, I'd have to tell her the reason. The truth is, I don't know how much time we have left.

Until she is officially in remission, we can't be sure that she's not going to get sick again and maybe this time she won't get better. I guess no one really knows how much time they have on earth. You could get hit by a car or struck by lightning or get cancer at any point. But just knowing that one of those three things is less likely to happen would make me feel a lot better. That's not the sort of depressing thing you want to discuss with your mother, especially if she's the one with the cancer. And so I smile and pretend everything is great and life is exciting. I don't complain when people come traipsing through our house all day long.

Part of the problem is that Mom is always willing to hear other people's problems. You would think she'd get enough of that, as a stylist and the best friend of woe-is-me Denise, but she can't say no to a weepy person, even after hours. So when by some miracle we find ourselves alone at dinner, I decide to approach the Doug thing.

"So," I begin. "Doug seems nice."

"He is nice," Mom says evenly, but the way she smiles says even more.

"You've been spending a lot of time with him, but I guess that's normal, since he's your personal trainer and everything."

"Yes," Mom agrees. "Training for a marathon takes up a lot of time."

I seriously doubt that accompanying the trainer for walks with his dog and having long phone conversations counts as marathon training. But I don't say that aloud. Instead I ask, "Is he a good trainer?"

"Very good; he keeps us all in stitches."

"Shouldn't he be concentrating on preparing you for the marathon?"

"Yes, but if you're not having fun, what's the point?"

"I thought the point was to raise money for cancer research."

"Yes, and also to have fun, get fit, and try new things."

"Has he done this kind of thing before?" I ask.

"What? Train people for marathons? It is one of the things a personal trainer does, Clarissa, yes. Where are you going with this?"

I can see I'm not going to get anywhere with this line of questioning. I decide to change tactics.

"Does he work long hours?"

Mom shrugs. "Not really. He's one of the top trainers at the gym. He makes his own schedule."

"So he can spend more time with his wife?"

Mom puts her fork down and looks right at me. "Stop."

I feign surprise. "Stop what? Doug is obviously someone who is important to you. Why shouldn't I want to know about him?"

Mom picks up her fork and resumes eating. "He's not married."

"Divorced?"

"Clarissa, that is none of your business."

"Is it yours?"

Mom sighs. "Spit it out, Clarissa."

"Spit what out?"

"Whatever it is you're trying to get at."

"Fine." But I don't ask right away. I scrape what's left of the potatoes off my plate, shove them into my mouth, chew, swallow, and then I think some more.

"Well? I don't have all day."

"Why? Do you have a date or something?" I ask innocently.

Mom looks at me and says slowly and precisely, as if she's

been practising it, "No, I do not have a date *tonight*. And if you had asked in the first place, I would have told you that Doug asked me to dinner and I said yes. So eventually, yes, I will have a date."

With that, she gets up, takes my plate, and starts clearing the table.

"But I'm not finished," I say.

"Oh yes you are."

Mom does the dishes in silence. She doesn't even turn on the radio, like she usually does. I slink off to watch TV in the den, but I can still feel her anger radiating down the hall and ruining my shows. I don't see why she's so upset when she's the one who is changing everything by bringing Doug into our lives. For someone who complains about there never being enough hours in the day, she seems to be able to make time for him.

Make Over

"Did you hear about Min's birthday party? She invited to whole class to her parents' restaurant. THE WHOLE CLASS!"

"I heard you, Mattie."

"She's so lucky. Her parents are going to close the Golden Dragon so it will be just us. After dinner, Min said we can push the tables back and have a dance. Can you imagine? Our own private dance!"

I don't really care for dances, but I do love the Golden Dragon. I especially love those crunchy orange noodles they give you for your won ton soup.

"Do you think everyone will come?" I ask. "Lots of people don't go to the school dances."

"This is different," Mattie insists. "It's a free all-you-can-eat buffet and a dance. Even the boys can't say no to that." She has a point. I have never known any boy to turn down a free dinner.

"Come on, let's go plan our outfits!" Mattie likes nothing more than putting outfits together. For a split second, I feel bad doing anything clothing-related without Benji, who watches those makeover shows religiously and is always honest about what looks good on you and what doesn't. But then I figure he gets to act on stage in a musical and wear real costumes, so I don't feel so guilty anymore. Still, Mattie and I have very different styles; I'm not sure I can trust someone who only wears jeans on Fridays.

"Maybe some other time," I say. "Benji will want to help out."

"Oh." Mattie struggles to look like she doesn't care.

Not wanting to hurt her feelings, I make her the perfect counter-offer. "Why don't you both come over after school on Friday? Then we can decide together."

That perks her up. "Okay! Do you think we could ask your mom to do our hair?"

I shrug. "Sure. She'll probably love that."

"Great! What are you going to get Min for her birthday?"

"I don't know, I haven't really thought —"

"Oh! We should go to the mall together. Maybe we can find outfits, too!"

"I wasn't really planning on getting a whole new outfit."

"Then we'll have to see what we can come up with. This is going to be the best party of the year, I just know it!"

***

By Friday, Mattie is so excited *I'm* ready to scream. She hasn't been able to talk about anything else. Luckily Benji is here and I can zone out for the skirt talk.

"So . . . I was thinking about wearing my jean skirt — you know, the one with the rainbow stitching? — but I don't think it's special enough for a dance. It's more of a casual everyday skirt. So then I thought maybe my purple skirt with the striped top, which I've only worn once —"

"For picture day," Benji says.

"Exactly! And then, like, if Josh and I start dating or whatever, obviously we'll trade school photos, and I'll be wearing the same outfit I wore when he first realized we should be together."

Benji looks impressed. Apparently he has never realized the full-blown magnitude of Mattie's craziness. I, however, have had weeks of one-on-one, undiluted Mattie-time.

"Wow, you've really thought this through," he says.

Mattie smiles. "Thanks."

"Do you really think that boys notice that stuff?" I ask.

"He will if I point it out," Mattie says.

Up in my bedroom, I allow Mattie and Benji to dissect my wardrobe. Benji finds an old pair of jeans that have gone soft in the knees and holds them out, frowning. I think they must have been blue once, but now they are sort of whitish-grey, like someone took a giant eraser and rubbed out all of the colour.

"Do these even fit you anymore?" he asks.

"Probably not."

Mattie spreads a knitted poncho with fraying tassels on the bed. There's a gaping hole near the corner where it looks like something may have been nibbling on the yarn. "What about this? When have you ever worn this?"

"I think it was a gift," I say.

Mattie rolls her eyes. "Oh, Clarissa. What are we going to do with you? You need to weed out your closet every season to make room for new pieces."

"Don't bother," Benji says. "I've been trying to tell her that for years."

"Hey! I weed!"

Benji is sceptical. "Oh, yeah? Name one thing you've thrown out this year."

I wrack my brains. There has to be something. "I had these reindeer pyjamas —"

"Pyjamas don't count," Mattie says.

"Besides you've had them for five years," Benji adds. "What else?"

"Some socks, some underwear . . ."

Mattie is scandalized. "Clarissa! Everyone throws out underwear! At least I hope they do . . ."

Benji grins wickedly. "Clarissa probably has underwear in here from grade three."

"That's disgusting!" Mattie giggles.

I reach into my sock drawer and throw a pair of balled-up socks in their direction. "Catch!"

Mattie squeals as the socks bounce off her shoulder and fall into Benji's lap. Benji unfolds them and pulls a sock over his hand. His thumb fits through a hole in the bottom. He wiggles it at Mattie, which makes her laugh even harder.

"See? She's hopeless."

Mattie looks at me, eyes shining. There is something suspicious about that glint in her eyes. "Clarissa, will you please let me — no, us —" she says, grabbing Benji's arm. "Will you please let us dress you for Min's party?"

"You can consider it your early birthday gift to me," Benji says.

"And me!" Mattie adds. "Please, please pretty please?"

I don't know. On one hand, it means I won't have to worry about picking my own outfit. On the other hand, I don't want to end up wearing one of Mattie's plaid jumpers or ruffled blouses in front of the whole class. This could go horribly, horribly wrong.

But it's very hard to say no to your two best friends when they are sitting there smiling and begging. Besides, it might just be the easiest present I ever give them.

"Fine," I say. "But it doesn't mean I'm going to like it."

"You don't have to like it," Benji says. "You just have to wear it."

* * *

After much deliberation, a snack, and two bathroom breaks, Mattie and Benji have finally decided on my outfit for Min's birthday. Before unveiling the winning selection, Mattie and Benji describe their process.

"First of all," Benji says, "we wanted to pick something that you would be comfortable in."

"Something that shows the real you," Mattie explains.

"Right. But we also thought you should step out of your comfort zone a little and try something new."

"Sooo, without further ado, drum roll please . . ." Benji drums his hands against his legs as Mattie throws open my closet door and my party outfit is revealed.

"Ta-da!"

At first I can't say anything. It is exactly what they promised it would be — me but with a twist.

Benji looks at me hopefully. "Well? What do you think? I know you don't like skirts, but that's why we paired it with the leggings, so it feels like you're wearing pants."

Along with black tights and a plain jean skirt that must belong to Mattie, they've added my favourite t-shirt, the one with an image of Dorothy from *The Wizard of Oz* movie silkscreened on the front, along with a short-sleeved red blouse. There isn't a hint of a ruffle or bow anywhere.

"You're supposed to wear the blouse unbuttoned," Mattie explains, "so you can see the t-shirt. I know you love t-shirts. That one is so vintage, which is very in right now."

"So you see? It's you, but the best version of you," says Benji proudly.

"If you're feeling extra-adventurous, you could add a cool scarf," Mattie suggests.

"Or dangly earrings!" says Benji.

"What about shoes?" I ask.

"You could wear a pair of mine," Mattie suggests. "I brought three pairs to choose from."

All of Mattie's shoes are shiny, glittery, or pink. I can't go to a party in shoes like that, I wouldn't feel like me. I reach into my closet and pull out my two-tone sneakers. They may not be pretty, but they're my favourites.

"What about these?"

"Perfect!" Mattie says. "Tights and sneakers go really well together."

"I love it," I admit. "I really, really love it." I feel guilty for second-guessing my friends. Scarf or no scarf, it is the best possible outfit and I never would have come up with it all by myself.

Mattie and Benji jump up and down, cheering and clapping. "High-five!" Mattie cries. Benji slaps his palm against hers and the two of them hug, congratulating themselves.

"We could go into business!" Mattie gushes.

"We could have our own show!" Benji says.

As they brainstorm names for their reality-based fashion 911 TV show I take one more glance in the mirror. For the first time, I'm really excited about the party.

Pair

Benji, Mattie, and I walk over to the Golden Dragon together. By the time we get there, half the class has already arrived. Min's mom meets us at the front door and checks our names off a list.

"Clarissa and Mattie, you'll both be at table six. Benjamin, you'll be at table two."

"Thanks, Mrs. Lu," Mattie says brightly.

"But —"

Mattie grabs my arm and pulls me in before I can finish.

"What are you doing?" I pull my arm back. "I was going to ask about the seating plan. Do you think she's serious?"

"Of course she's serious," Mattie whispers. "People take seating plans very seriously. You don't want to be rude."

"But I always sit with Benji," I insist.

"You'll be fine, right Benji? It's not like you don't know these people."

"I guess." Benji looks unconvinced.

"Maybe you can switch with someone, Benji," I suggest.

"Hi guys! Thanks for coming! Did you get your seating assignments?" Min asks. She is all dolled-up in an outfit that makes her look a little bit like a pop star and a little bit like a Barbie doll. I'm not sure which part I dislike more.

"About that —" I start, but Min leans in and giggles.

"You can thank me later," she says, and then rushes off to say hello to someone else.

"Is it just me, or was that weird?" I ask.

"Definitely weird," Benji agrees. "Well, I guess I should go over to my table now."

"Don't worry, I'll come visit," I promise.

The restaurant is full. Someone has turned the stereo up and groups of girls are singing along and shuffling to the music, tossing their hair and throwing their arms up and giggling like mad. I recognize the song but I'm not really into dancing in front of people. I edge toward the buffet, which is an array of covered dishes that smell tantalizingly delicious. I am considering taking a peek under one of the lids when Min's dad turns up right beside me.

"Hungry?" Mr. Lu asks.

I blush. "A little," I say. Thank goodness the lights are dimmed.

Mr. Lu smiles at me. "Dinner is soon enough. Go, dance!" He shoos me toward the makeshift dance floor. Reluctantly I make my way over to the edge of the circle of girls Mattie has joined.

Somehow I get through the next ten minutes, nodding my head and smiling whenever someone says to me, "how much do you love this song?" Finally, Mr. Lu turns the music down and announces that dinner is served.

I pile my plate with egg rolls, chow mein, and plenty of sweet-and-sour chicken. Behind me, Mattie hems and haws over the vegetarian options, spooning little mouthfuls onto her plate.

"Is that all you're going to eat?" I ask.

"I don't want to pig out in front of Josh," Mattie whispers.

"I thought you were a feminist," I say.

Mattie looks torn. "'It's a buffet, I can always get seconds," she compromises.

I plop another chicken ball onto the mound of food on my plate, like a delicious fried cherry on top of a sundae made of rice and stir-fried vegetables. "Suit yourself."

There are six people at each table. It becomes clear that the seating arrangements are definitely not random. Mattie and I are at a table with Michael, Josh, Chudy, and Amanda. In front of each place is a name card, carefully lettered in glittery pen. The arrangement is boy–girl, boy–girl. I'm seated between Michael and Chudy. We've been paired off in some sort of romantic matchmaking attempt.

I should have known Min would pull a stunt like this. Mattie hasn't been exactly secretive about her obsession with Josh, and Amanda Krespi has been in love with Chudy Adeyemi ever since he won the countywide public-speaking contest last year. I can understand why; even I have to admit, he has the nicest speaking voice of any kid I know. He presented on global farming practices, and I managed to stay awake for the whole thing. Clearly Min is trying to play matchmaker; so what does it mean that she put me next to Michael? Does she think I like Michael? Did Mattie say something to her?

Or worse, did Michael say something about me?

Thank goodness I took so much food. I have so much to eat that no one could possibly expect me to contribute to the conversation, which is awkward at best.

"Well, this is certainly nice of Min's parents, isn't it? It's very classy, just what I would want for my birthday party," says Mattie. She has already finished her four mouthfuls of food and is desperately trying to engage someone, anyone, in conversation.

Chudy nods and swallows. "Yes, it's very nice," he says politely.

"When's your birthday, Chudy?" Mattie asks.

Immediately, Amanda says, "May twenty-first." She flushes the minute the words fly out of her mouth. "I — I remember because last year we sang happy birthday to you early because we were off for Victoria Day on your real birthday." Amanda smiles weakly and looks around the table for someone to rescue her. "Remember?"

Chudy, always the gentleman, smiles politely at Amanda. "Yes, that's true," he says.

Mattie laughs; a little too loudly, if you ask me. "I remember! Amanda you have such a great memory."

Amanda smiles gratefully at her. It's a nice save, but a little too late. The crazy is already out there for everyone to see. Mattie turns to Josh and, in a remarkable display of coolness, manages to ask him about his birthday without blushing or squealing.

"August," he replies.

"It must be hard having a summer birthday," she says. "Everyone's always away."

Josh shrugs. "I usually bring a friend up to my cottage and we go tubing or something."

"That sounds amazing! I love water sports!" Mattie gushes.

I am fairly certain the only water sport Mattie Cohen has taken part in is swimming, and that was at an all-girls summer camp where it didn't matter if your hair was tangled or turned green from too much chlorine. I can practically see the wheels in her head turning, imagining herself as the guest of honour at Josh's cottage, decked out in her flowered bikini and those big pink sunglasses of hers.

"Cool," says Josh.

"Do you have a canoe at your cottage?" Mattie asks.

"Yup."

"I took canoeing at camp last year," Amanda chimes in. She sneaks a glance at Chudy and asks him "Have you ever canoed, Chudy?"

"No," he says.

"Personally, I think kayaking is way better," Michael says.

"Yeah, we've got a couple of kayaks, too," Josh says.

Cripes. Has there ever been a more boring conversation? I'm about to excuse myself and hit up the buffet for a second round when Michael looks at me and says, "What about you? Have you ever kayaked, Clarissa?"

"No," I admit. "I'm not really into water sports. Or any sports really."

Mattie laughs. "Oh, Clarissa! Don't be so modest!"

"It's true," I insist. "I might as well be allergic to sports."

"You're pretty good at badminton," Michael says.

I don't know who is more surprised, me or Mattie. I avoid looking in her direction, but out of the corner of my eye I can see her eyebrows are raised and she is most definitely sending me an I Told You So look.

"It's not like it's one of the hard sports," I mutter.

"I like badminton," Josh says.

"Me, too! Oh my gosh! I just had the best idea. We should play mixed doubles in the badminton tournament!"

Josh, Michael, and I stare at Mattie with blank expressions on our faces. "The what?" I ask.

Mattie rolls her eyes. "You know, the senior badminton tournament? At lunch hour? It's in two weeks?" When none of us shows even the slightest glimmer of recognition, Mattie huffs and exclaims, "Am I the only one who listens to morning announcements?"

"No, I remember something about that," Chudy says.

Mattie smiles gratefully at him. "Well? What do you think?"

Mattie looks from me to Josh to Michael expectantly. I feel bad, but competitive sports, even badminton, really aren't my thing. Josh starts digging around his chicken fried rice. The silence is becoming unbearably long until Michael pipes up.

"Sure," he says. "I'm in. Clarissa?" Michael is looking right at me. If you've ever had someone look straight into your eyes you know how difficult it can be to look away, especially if that someone has particularly nice eyes, blue with a little bit of green, like those cat's eye marbles.

Suddenly my throat feels dry and I have to clear it a few times before I'm able to speak. "Okay, but only if Josh plays, too."

Josh shrugs. "Whatever."

"Great! So it's settled! I'll sign us up on Monday. Clarissa will play with Michael and I'll play with Josh!" Mattie should be over the moon excited, but her voice sounds a little strained and she's in such a hurry to leave the table that she almost knocks the chair over as she stands and rushes over to the buffet. I get up to follow her.

At the buffet, I lean over and whisper, "Pretty smooth, huh?" Mattie turns her back to me and roots through the pile of chicken balls. I tap her shoulder. "Hello? I said that was pretty smooth."

Mattie whirls around, nostrils flaring and an angry flush creeping up her neck toward her cheeks. "You know, sometimes you can be really mean!"

"What?"

"You heard me."

71

"I heard you, but I don't get it."

"Oh, yeah, right. What was all that 'only if Josh plays' business?"

"Nothing! I just wanted to make sure he got the message."

"Oh, he got the message all right. Him and everyone else at the table."

"CRIPES, Mattie, what are you talking about? Why can't you talk like a normal person?"

Mattie's jaw drops. "You're the one who isn't normal, Clarissa! You know how much I like Josh. I can't believe you would do that to me, or to Michael."

"What does Michael have to do with anything?"

But Mattie stomps away and pulls up a chair at Min's table. Fine, if she wants to be that way then it's her choice. I head back to table six and try to ignore the sound of Mattie sniffing.

Oops

After dinner, the music comes back on. People start mingling again. There is less dancing, thank goodness, probably because people are too full to do much in the way of moving. Mattie is sitting in a corner sniffing into a napkin and surrounded by girls. Every once in a while she looks across the room at me with her weepy red eyes. Whenever I catch her glance she bursts into fresh bouts of wailing. Cripes.

When no one's looking, I grab Benji and pull him into the women's washroom.

"Boy are you in trouble," Benji whispers.

"Why? What did I do?" I cry.

"She thinks you're trying to steal Josh from her."

"What?"

"Shh!" Benji looks around frantically before pulling me into a stall, locking the door behind us. "What if someone finds us? I'm not supposed to be in here."

I make a concerted effort to lower my voice. "That's the most ridiculous thing I've ever heard. Why does she think that?"

Benji shrugs. "Apparently you said you would only play badminton if Josh plays."

"So?"

Benji looks disappointed, but not all that surprised. "It's true? You actually said that?"

73

"I guess, but I was doing it for her benefit."

Benji shakes his head. "Oh, Clarissa, don't you see? You made it sound like the only reason you're playing is because Josh is playing, so now Mattie thinks you like him."

I am aghast. "What? That's not it at all! I just said that so Josh would have to play! I did it for her sake!"

Benji pats my shoulder. "I know that, but Mattie doesn't, and Michael probably doesn't either."

"I don't care what Michael thinks," I say, maybe a little too quickly. Benji says nothing. "Anyway, what do I do now? How do I convince Mattie that she's being a crazy drama queen and that she can have stupid Josh Simmons?"

"First of all, I wouldn't put it that way. Second of all, you should just tell her," he says simply.

"That's what I tried to do before but she stomped off and cried her eyes out to anyone who would listen!"

Benji smiles sympathetically. "You may have to try a few times."

***

A few times is an understatement. I decide to give her some room for the rest of the party. Even if I wanted to approach her, I'd have to make my way through an army of girls who are protecting her from the likes of me.

Instead I flop on a chair next to Benji and listen to him rattle on about rehearsal and his new artsy friends. "Charity was telling us about this audition she had once where she had to eat a bowl of pink cereal. It turned out she was allergic to the dye in the cereal and her throat swelled shut and she had to be rushed to the hospital. The casting director sent her flowers and now she gets an audition for every one of his commercials. Isn't that amazing?"

74

"Mmm." It's not that I don't care about Charity Smith-Jones and her fabulous acting career, I just don't care to hear about it every spare moment I get to spend with Benji. He's only known her a few weeks. We've been friends forever. I wonder if he bores her to death with stories about me. Probably not.

"Can I sit with you guys?" Michael drags a chair and joins us at the edge of the dance floor. Across the room, Mattie and her bodyguards shake their heads and start whispering furiously.

"What's with them?" Michael asks, nodding in their direction.

"Who knows," I lie. "It's probably nothing."

"Mattie thinks Clarissa likes Josh," Benji blurts out.

I don't know who is redder, me or Michael. The last thing I want is for him to see me blushing. I shouldn't have worried, Michael is looking down at his shoes. "Oh," he manages.

"But I don't!" I say quickly. "I don't like him. Mattie does. I just wanted to make sure he signed up for badminton. For her sake."

"Oh," Michael says. "That's good. I mean, that's nice of you to do. For Mattie."

Benji looks like he's about to bolt but I don't think I could sit here and talk to Michael all by myself, so I do the only thing I can think of to get him to stay put. "So, Benji was telling me about rehearsals. Did you know he's playing the Cowardly Lion in *The Wizard of Oz*?"

"For real? Like, singing and dancing and everything?" Michael asks.

Benji nods, blushing with pleasure. "I think it's going to be really good," he gushes. "Just wait till you see our

Dorothy." He launches into one of his many Charity stories, which I know practically by heart, but this time it doesn't bother me so much.

Michael is genuinely interested. "When is it?" he asks.

"At the end of May," Benji says casually, as if he hasn't been crossing off the days on his calendar every night.

"Cool. Do I get tickets from you?"

Benji is elated. "Sure! Or you can call the box office or else buy them in person at Flowers Plus — that's where the assistant director works during the week."

"When are you going, Clarissa?"

Benji and I exchange glances. In all the Wizard talk, this is one thing we haven't discussed yet. "Probably opening night, but maybe closing. Or both. I haven't decided."

"Well, when you decide, let me know. I'll come that night, too."

"Sure," I say. Is this a date? Is Michael asking me out on a date? Does it count as a date if the boy suggests it but you have to call him and tell him when and where?

"Mattie will probably be there, too," I say. "That is if she's speaking to me at that point."

"That's cool, maybe we can all sit together. We'll be your own personal fan club, Benji."

Benji smiles. "Cool," he repeats. We lapse into silence, Benji looking all dopey and starry-eyed, probably contemplating what it will feel like to have groupies; Michael helping himself to a half-eaten slice of birthday cake that someone left at the table; and me wondering whether or not I've just agreed to go on a date with Michael Greenblat.

Solo

Apparently Mattie wasn't going to let the whole Josh Simmons thing blow over, because at lunch on Monday, she sat with Amanda and Min instead of at our usual table with Benji.

"You still haven't apologized?" Benji asks.

"Not really," I admit.

"You should go over there and do it before it gets worse."

"And give Min and Amanda the satisfaction of seeing me grovel? Never."

"You don't have to do it in front of them."

"I don't think I should have to apologize at all."

"But Mattie does."

"Fine." I down the rest of my juice box and stomp over to the table where Min, Amanda, and Mattie are sitting. Min and Amanda stop talking and Mattie refuses to look up at me.

"Hey," I say. All three of them give me the silent treatment. "I said *hey*," I repeat. Still nothing. "Mattie, can I talk to you for a second?"

Mattie straightens up but still refuses to look me in the eye. "About what?"

"You know about what. Can you just please come back to the table for a second?"

Mattie sniffs. "Anything you have to say to me can be said in front of Min and Amanda."

I grit my teeth and tell myself to remain calm. "Look, I know you're still mad at me, but believe me when I say I don't like Josh and I would never do anything to stop you from dating him, if that's what you really want."

"So you admit you knew that I liked Josh all along?" Mattie asks.

"Yes, obviously."

"And you admit that what you said was hurtful and uncalled for?"

"Now wait a minute, you're the one who took it the wrong way. You're the one who overreacted!"

Amanda gasps and Min shakes her head. Mattie looks right at me, her cheeks turning pink with anger. She is madder than I've ever seen her before. "Overreacted?"

"Yes, overreacted," I repeat. "I said I was sorry, can't we just get over this?"

"Actually, I don't recall you using the word sorry."

"Fine. I'm sorry, Mattie. I didn't mean it and you know it. I'm very, very sorry."

"You have to mean it when you say it, Clarissa, otherwise it doesn't count."

Amanda rolls her eyes at Min and I am tempted to reach over and slap the smug looks off both of their faces. Mattie is making me look stupid on purpose. I am sorry, but right now I am also pissed off.

"Can we please talk about this alone?" I say between gritted teeth.

"Actually, I think I'm done talking about this," Mattie says, and she turns away from me.

I make my way back to Benji, fuming.

78

"I take it that didn't go well," he says.

I help myself to his chips, stuffing them in my mouth by the handful to keep from screaming.

"You can always try again tomorrow," Benji suggests.

***

I don't get a chance to talk to Mattie on Tuesday either, though I go out of my way to catch her eye and smile at her in class. Each time she pretends not to see me, tossing her hair over one shoulder. I even stoop so low as to write her a note, entrusting it to Benji to pass along in Geography.

"Did she say anything about the note?" I ask after class.

Benji shakes his head, no. "Sorry, Clarissa. I don't even know if she read it — she just stuffed it in her backpack."

I'm not the kind of person who thinks it is acceptable to apologize in letter form. In my note, I told Mattie I was really and truly sorry and I wanted the chance to say so in person. But first she has to acknowledge my presence.

On Thursday after school, I wait for Mattie at her locker like I always do, but after waiting for fifteen minutes it dawns on me that she isn't going to show. She's gone home without me. All of a sudden I can't get out of there fast enough. I walk home alone, head down, shocked at how mad Mattie is. I know she likes Josh and everything, but this seems extreme, even for Mattie.

At home, I turn on the TV and the radio, and walk from room to room turning on all the lights. I'm too restless to do anything else. Mom is at the gym with her running team and Doug, Benji's at rehearsal, and Mattie is at home eating her healthy snack and singing along to Sheryl Crow and Sarah McLachlan without me. I stare at the phone, willing it to ring.

Finally it dawns on me that I'm the one who has to pick up the phone. Mattie's is one of only three phone numbers that I know by heart. Maybe I should tell her that. Surely it'll count for something.

"Hello?"

"Hi Cheryl, it's Clarissa. Can I speak to Mattie, please?"

There is a pause and the sound of muffled voices, and then Cheryl says, "I'm sorry, Clarissa, she isn't in the mood to talk right now. Can I take a message?"

I swallow, wondering if Mattie has told her mother about our fight. She probably hates me. I can't say that I blame her. I hate me a little right now, too. "Would you please tell her that I called to say I'm sorry and that I really, really mean it."

"Yes, Clarissa. I'll tell her. Have a good night."

Doubtful.

Mend

The Sunday before the tournament, Mattie finally returns my calls. It seems the tournament is still a go, and she has decided that we need to brush up on our badminton skills.

"What skills?" I ask. "It's badminton."

"Don't you want to win?" Mattie asks.

"I guess." I don't care so much about the tournament. I'm only doing it to win Mattie back. This past week was horrible. I had no idea how much I liked Mattie until she refused to talk to me. With Benji always at rehearsal and my mother spending every spare second with Doug, it feels like I'm losing people left, right, and centre. I don't want to lose her, too.

We agree to meet at Mattie's place after lunch. Benji is at rehearsal (of course) and I've done as much of my homework as I'm likely to do, so I'm as free as a bird. It's one of those spring days that feels more like summer. It seems like the whole world is out, gardening or walking or just finding reasons to be about, smiling in the sunshine.

I ring Mattie's doorbell, hoping to avoid her mother. Even though I know I'm not at fault and Mattie claims to have forgiven me, I still feel low-down about the whole thing. I don't like the idea of other people's parents thinking bad things about me.

"Clarissa!" Just my luck, Cheryl Cohen opens the door. By the way she says my name, I can tell she knows about our fight. I smile at her and pray to whoever's listening that she doesn't ask me to talk about it. The Cohens love to talk things through.

Cheryl is smiling at me expectantly, waiting for me to volunteer information. No, thank you! Mattie's mom has never been anything but perfectly nice to me but I'm uncomfortable about how much she knows about my family. She was my mother's nurse after her surgery and has seen both Mom and me at what should be the most private of times. I guess in most cases your nurse is a person you never expect to see again, so you can cry, curse, or do any number of embarrassing things and it's like they never happened. But Mattie had to go and ingratiate herself into my life and now I see her mother at least once a week.

When it becomes abundantly clear that my lips are remaining sealed, Cheryl gives my shoulder a squeeze and says, "Mattie's in the backyard waiting for you. Go on."

I smile and thank Cheryl but not before she pulls me in for a quick hug and says directly into my ear, "I'm glad you two made up." I mumble something between thank you and see you later and get myself out of that situation lickety-split.

In the backyard, I find Mattie bouncing a birdie on a brand new racquet. I hang back, unsure of what to say. This is the first time we've hung out together since Min's party, which already feels like a million years ago. I am about to launch into another apology when Mattie spots me, smiles, and says, "There you are! I'm just testing for the sweet spot."

"The what?"

"The sweet spot is the part of the racquet you want to hit the birdie with," she explains, sounding suspiciously like a text book. "You want to avoid hitting it off the frame, which is called a wood shot."

I pick up the extra racquet that's leaning against the deck. Nothing about it looks wooden. "Why is it called a wood shot?"

"Because the frame is wooden. Well not that particular racquet, it's aluminum, but originally all racquets were made of wood."

"Is aluminum better than wood?"

Mattie shrugs. "I don't know. It's the only kind they had at Canadian Tire," she admits.

"How do you know so much about badminton?" I ask.

"I looked it up. Here, I printed you a copy of the rules." Mattie hands me a neatly stapled stack of paper with paragraphs cut and pasted from different websites. I can't think of anything more boring than reading about badminton.

"This is at least ten pages," I say.

"So?"

"I just want to play badminton; I don't want to read about it."

"This will give us an advantage!" Mattie says. "Don't you want to know everything about something before you go ahead and do it?"

This is where Mattie and I differ. I prefer not to think about something and hope that everything turns out for the best. If I knew everything about something then I'd for sure find a reason not to do it. Last year, Mr. Campbell read us a poem about two roads diverging in a wood. He said whenever we find ourselves at an impasse in life we should think about those two paths and really consider our options. What he really meant was, take the path less chosen. You can bet that before she takes any path, Mattie Cohen has consulted every possible map and GPS device, written a pros and cons list, and conducted a poll. Today, badminton was her path, and I was along for the ride.

"Can't you just tell me the stuff I need to know?" I ask.

Mattie bristles and stands a little stiffer. She gets prissy when she's angry. I'm not exactly out of the doghouse yet, so I make an effort to soften her up. "Fine, I'll read it tonight, but for now, can you just give me a rundown of the basics?"

Mattie's shoulders relax and she downshifts into teaching mode, which is one of her favourite states of being.

Half an hour later I'm so anxious I feel like my entire body is made of the strings on a badminton racquet, stretched tight and ready to go. There are a lot of rules in badminton. It always looked so simple to me, but apparently there are infractions, techniques, and strategies to consider. I'm almost certain I'll never remember them all. Knowing Mattie, there is probably a test at the end of all this.

"So, did you get all that?"

Hallelujah! I jump to my feet and grab my racquet. "Yep!" I lie. "Let's play!"

It is one of the sad truths in life that just because you have read everything there is to read about something, it doesn't mean you will be any good at it. Poor Mattie might be the worst badminton player I have ever seen. She flails about, sending the birdie everywhere but toward me. Once she actually hit the birdie backwards over her own head.

"You know," Mattie puffs, "a lot of people think badminton is just an easier version of tennis, but actually badminton is more aerobically challenging."

I would like to agree, but I'm too busy trying to catch my breath from running all over the backyard after Mattie's wild serves. After several deep breaths I am able to huff out a few words. "Can . . . we . . . take . . . a . . . break?"

Mattie frowns. "Don't you think we should keep practising?" In response, I drop my racquet and flop onto the grass.

"Okay, fine. But just for five minutes. I'll go get us a drink."

I close my eyes, fling out my arms and legs, and wait for the earth to stop tilting. From above I must look like a human X marking the spot on some aerial treasure hunt. I take deep, slow breaths, inhaling the smell of new grass. A light breeze cools the sweat on my skin, and I can feel the full-body flush draining back into my body, where it came from. I feel tired and sore and relaxed and full of energy all at once. I really should exercise more.

Something is blocking my sun.

"Here you go." I open one eye to see Mattie standing over me holding out a glass of water.

"Water?" I say. I am unable to keep the disappointment out of my voice. I was hoping for lemonade or root beer or something with a little kick to it.

Mattie nods. "It's good for you."

I sit up and take the glass. Mattie sits beside me and we down our good-for-you waters in silence. I like the way the coolness of the water spreads throughout my body. Finally the sound of my own blood pounding in my ears has all but disappeared and my heart is beating at a more peaceful pace. All those endorphins I whipped up during badminton are telling me that now is the time to bring up the birthday fiasco.

I have to clear my throat a few times before I can get the words out. Endorphins or not, apologizing is never easy.

"I just wanted to say, again, that I'm sorry about the party. I didn't even know I was going to say what I said, I didn't plan it, and I didn't mean anything by it. At all." Phew. There.

Mattie narrows her eyes at me. "So you don't have any interest in Josh?"

I suppress the urge to shudder. "Not at all."

"And you weren't trying to humiliate me on purpose?"

I think the word humiliate is a little strong, but I keep that to myself. "Of course not! Why would I do that?"

Mattie shakes her head. "I don't know, sometimes you are a closed book, Clarissa. I don't know what you're thinking."

"So you immediately assume I'm always thinking something cruel?"

Mattie sighs. "No."

"Well, then? You really think I would go after someone you like? Just to be mean?"

"No, I guess not. But some girls would."

"Not me."

Mattie smiles. "You're right. Not you. I'm sorry. I guess I overreacted a little."

A little? Now there's the understatement of the year. But I let it go. I'm just relieved that we can go back to being friends again. "So, we're good?"

Mattie jumps up and offers me her hand. Reluctantly, I let her pull me to my feet. "Better than good, we're great," she says. "Now let's go over a few more serving techniques and we'll be ready for the tournament. I included a diagram on page five of your package."

Cripes.

Team

I guess badminton isn't much of a spectator sport, and for that I am grateful. When we arrive in the gym there are handfuls of people hanging around the bleachers. The gym is divided into four separate badminton courts. Mattie consults the schedule and discovers that she and Josh are playing in the first round but Michael and I aren't playing until round two.

"Perfect," she says. "That way we can cheer each other on."

Michael and Josh smile at her, but neither of them looks too thrilled about playing cheerleader.

"Good luck," I say.

Mattie throws her arms around my neck and gives me one of her full-body hugs. "Thanks!"

Benji waves and calls out from the stands, "Break a leg!"

The boys shake hands and Michael and I take seats next to Benji.

"Was that right? Can I say break a leg, or is that bad luck?" Benji asks.

"How could it be bad luck?" says Michael.

"In theatre it's bad luck to wish someone good luck," Benji explains. "That's why actors always tell each other to break a leg."

"Oh," says Michael. "I don't think it matters in sports. People are always wishing each other good luck."

"But people are always breaking bones and getting injuries in sports," Benji points out.

"I never thought of it that way," Michael admits.

It turns out Mattie and Josh are going to need a lot more than luck to win their round. Mattie uses her racquet as a shield more than anything else, desperately batting at the birdie as if it's attacking her. If I didn't know any better, I'd think she was afraid of it.

"I thought you said you practised," Benji whispers.

"We did," I insist.

Every time she misses a shot, Mattie apologizes and tries to laugh it off, tossing her hair in a way she must think is fetching. One of these times she's going to get a crick in her neck. Josh smiles at her, but his smiles are getting tighter and tighter. I wish there was something I could do. Not only is Mattie going to lose the game, but she's probably going to lose any chance she had with Josh, too. I don't know very much about boys, but I do know they hate losing.

"I can't watch," I moan.

"You have to," Benji says. "Just keep smiling." He cups his hands around his mouth and calls, "Go, Mattie!"

Behind us, someone adds, "Yeah, go get some lessons."

I whip around and glare at the people behind us, who burst out laughing as Mattie ducks and the birdie bounces off her head. I glare at them and say, "Do you mind? I'm trying to watch."

"Is that your friend?" asks a boy with a red soccer shirt and matching shorts. He looks vaguely familiar.

"Yes," I say.

"Are you as bad as she is? If you are, then Claire and I are a shoo-in."

Red Shirt's friends laugh and Claire, a pretty girl with

freckles, a short, stubby ponytail, and three earrings in each ear smiles smugly at me.

"You think you can do better?" I scoff.

"Actually, I do," she says.

"Hey, Greenblat, is that your partner?" Red Shirt asks, nodding at me.

Michael blushes, which makes the boys whistle and Red Shirt grin.

"I didn't hear you, Greenblat."

"That's because he didn't say anything," I say.

Red Shirt narrows his eyes. "Well if that is your partner, you better hope her serve is as sharp as her mouth. We're up next. Come on, Claire."

Red Shirt and Claire stand up and walk between us, making sure to bump our shoulders as they pass.

"Who is that?" I ask.

"Wesley Turner," Michael answers.

"That name sounds familiar," I say.

"He's the captain of the basketball team," Michael says. He sounds miserable.

"So?" I shrug.

"So, that makes him kind of a big deal. In basketball season, anyway."

"Isn't basketball over?" I ask.

"Yes," Michael says.

"What does basketball have to do with badminton?"

Michael shrugs. "Nothing, I guess. I've just never seen him be bad at any sport. Ever."

"Well, we'll just have to show him," I say.

Michael looks doubtful. I rummage around in my gym bag and pull out Mattie's package of tips and strategies.

"Here's what we're going to do . . ."

* * *

I pass Mattie on the way to the court. Her cheeks are flushed, but I'm not sure if it's from embarrassment or all the running around. She manages to keep smiling, despite being squashed, twenty-one to three. Josh heads straight for the change room, head down.

"Good game, Josh!" she calls after him. He doesn't turn around. Mattie smiles weakly at me. "Don't take it personally. I'm sure he wants to cheer you on, but he's really tired. But don't worry, I'll be rooting for you!" She gives me a sweaty hug and I head off to the court to avenge the honour of my friend and Ferndale's worst badminton player.

Wesley "Red Shirt" Turner may be a good athlete, but thanks to Mattie, I am better prepared. I stay close to the net and Michael covers the back half of the court. He may have a more powerful serve than I do, but I am good at the sneaky ones that barely make it over the net to land just inside the line. Twice, Claire smirks at me and turns away from the birdie only to have it land right at her feet. After the third time, Michael whoops and offers his hand for a high-five.

"Nice one!" he says. It feels good to be on a winning team.

Wesley frowns and starts bossing Claire around. She's not as pretty when she's upset. I almost feel sorry for her.

Now the serves are coming fast and hard. In the bleachers, Mattie is cheering us on. My heart is pounding, my legs are burning, and there is sweat in my eyes; I'm loving every second of it. Imagine that: me, Clarissa Louise Delaney, enjoying sports.

"This is fun," I say to Michael.

He smiles back. "See? I was right. You *are* good at badminton." Just then the birdie whizzes by my ear, too close to be an accident. I flinch but Michael lunges and slams it back over the net. The air around my ear is still humming with the sound of the birdie connecting with the strings of the racquet.

"Watch it!" Michael says.

"You watch it," Wesley sneers. "Maybe you should pay more attention to the birdie and less to your partner."

"Sounds like someone's jealous," Michael calls.

Wesley's eyebrows go up and he gives me the once over. "Jealous? Of what? I don't see anything to be jealous about."

Wesley "Red Shirt" Turner is what my mother would call human lint, and why should I care what human lint thinks of me? This might be the only time in history that I am glad to be red and sweaty; at least no one can see me blush.

Claire laughs. "Yeah, Greenblat. You must have been really desperate if *this* is all you can find to double up with you."

That word, that *this*, hangs in the air between us like a bad smell. Any lingering feelings of empathy I had for Claire are totally gone. But before I can open my mouth to reply, Michael cuts in, "Actually, Clarissa's the only reason I'm playing in this stupid tournament. If you're lucky, maybe she'll give you a few tips after we kick your ass." And then he slams the birdie over the net, driving it right into the ground for the final point, like the sweetest exclamation mark at the end of an awesome sentence.

"GOTCHA!" I cry. "Nice one, Michael!"

Without even thinking, I drop my racquet and rush over and find myself in the middle of a hug with Michael Greenblat. Hugging a boy is not like hugging a girl. A girl smells like shampoo and hair gel and flavoured lip gloss, but Michael smells like clean laundry and hot dogs and something else I can't quite put my finger on. A girl will pull you in until you're squished together, but there is nothing squishy about hugging Michael. He is hard in all the places where Mattie is soft. His shirt under my hands is damp from badminton. As suddenly as it began, the hug is over, and I step back, feeling dazed.

In the bleachers, Mattie and Benji are clutching each other, jumping up and down, whooping and hollering. Across the court, Wesley is yelling at Claire for missing the shot, but she ignores him, pulling the elastic out of her ponytail and shaking out her hair, which lands in a cute, piecey little haircut, not a hair out place, no sign of frizz or that bump the elastic leaves in your hair when you take a ponytail out. Now I hate her even more. She glares at me on her way to the girls' change room, but I don't care because in front of me, Michael is smiling in his Michael way, with one side of his mouth twitching up, like he's trying not to smile. Something gushes through my veins and almost takes my breath away. I tell myself it's probably just the exercise endorphins.

***

For the next week, Michael and I spend the second half of our lunch hour totally annihilating the other badminton pairs. We've even attracted a crowd, if you can call ten people a crowd. Mattie is a true friend. Despite her embarrassing loss on the first day, she is front and centre for every match, leading cheers and happy to talk to anyone who will listen about how she taught me everything I know. I don't correct her. I figure it's almost true. Josh is not such a good sport. He doesn't come to a single one of our matches.

"What a poor loser," I complain.

Mattie jumps to his defence. "It's hard for boys to lose."

"It's just as hard for girls," I counter.

Benji agrees with Mattie. "It's not quite the same. Boys like Josh build their entire reputation on being good at sports. Look at my dad. He still talks about his glory days."

This is true. The Dentonator will often give us play-by-plays of his best games as if we were there in the arena with him, instead of years away from being born.

"And what about you?" I ask Benji. "You would never be such a sore loser."

"True," he agrees. "Then again, I am much more mature than most boys." I can't argue with that. Benji is more mature than most adults I know.

After winning six matches in a row, Michael and I are declared the undisputed Mixed Doubles Intramural Badminton Champions. For all of our badminton prowess, we are awarded blue ribbons with the school's crest stamped on them and two gift certificates to Pizza Hut.

"I love Pizza Hut!" Michael says. "When should we go? Are you free Saturday night?"

"I don't know," I say, and I pretend to think it over. The truth is I'm free most nights, now that Benji has his stupid musical and all of his stupid musical friends. "Yeah, I think that works."

"Cool. I'll meet you at seven. I wonder if this includes the sundae buffet."

Mattie waits until Michel is out of earshot before grabbing my arm and squealing in my ear. "Do you realize what just happened? Michael asked you on a date! I can't believe you're going on a date before I am. You don't even believe in love."

93

I roll my eyes. "This isn't about *love*, and it isn't a date. We won the gift certificates fair and square; it would be wasteful not to use them."

Now Mattie rolls her eyes at me. "Oh, please. Why can't you just admit that Michael asked you on a date, a real date, in a real restaurant —"

"I'm not sure if Pizza Hut counts as a real restaurant —"

"It does so count, and you're excited! Admit it!" Mattie demands.

"Fine. I am excited to eat free pizza in a restaurant with my badminton partner."

Mattie throws her hands up in exasperation.

"Now for the important part," Benji says. "What are you going to wear?"

Date?

I don't tell Mom about my maybe-date. Why should I? It's not like she's around long enough to hear about it. Between her clients, running, Denise, and now Doug, I feel like I never see her.

Besides, the more I think about it, the less it seems like a real date. Does it count as a date if the only reason the boy asks you is because you both won gift certificates? It's not like one of us could use them and not the other; we both earned them. Although I suppose it doesn't say anything about us using them together at the same time. I could very well have invited Benji and Michael could have asked one of his basketball friends. Still. Is it a date if the boy meets you at the restaurant instead of picking you up at the door? Mattie calls me just after six to check in.

"I told my mom I'm going to your house for dinner," I say.

On the other end of the line, Mattie sighs heavily. "You know I don't like lying," she says. "But if you pinkie-swear to come here straight after your date —"

"Maybe-date."

"— your DATE-DATE, then I guess it isn't exactly a lie."

"Good."

"What are you wearing?" she asks. Even over the phone,

I can hear the concern in her voice. Honestly. I'm almost fourteen years old; I am perfectly capable of picking out an outfit myself.

"I thought I would wear my badminton clothes, you know, like a tribute to our success."

"Ha, ha, very funny," Mattie says, clearly not amused.

"I just picked out something normal," I say. "I don't want to look like I'm trying too hard."

The truth is I tried on four or five different outfits before deciding on Mattie's skirt, which I still have from Min's party, tights, and one of my classic Clarissa t-shirts. This one I inherited from my mom. It's her old high school shirt, featuring a graphic of a fierce-looking badger wearing a football helmet. Apparently the Sir John A. Macdonald High School's mascot was a badger. Benji calls it my Hufflepuff shirt.

"Are you at least wearing a skirt?" Mattie asks.

"Yes, in fact I am wearing your skirt."

"Ooh, I love that skirt on you!" she gushes. "You know, you're getting so much wear out of it you should just keep it. I need a new one, anyway. That one's kind of out of style. No offense," she adds quickly. "It's just a little dated for me, but it totally suits your style."

That's a bit rich, coming from someone who almost exclusively wears Mary Janes with knee socks, and collared blouses buttoned up to the neck.

"Are you nervous?" Mattie asks.

"Not really."

"You're so lucky," she says wistfully.

A twinge of guilt twists in my belly. The only reason I agreed to play in the badminton tournament is because Mattie needed an excuse to do something with Josh. Now here I am, about to go on my first maybe-date, and Josh isn't talking to her. It doesn't seem right.

"Josh isn't worth it," I say. "Someone better will come along."

"You're right," Mattie sighs. "Someone better and someone older."

"Someone with nicer hair," I add.

"Someone who doesn't skateboard!" Mattie giggles. "Okay, I should go. Don't forget to bring gum for after dinner in case he tries to kiss you. Then you won't have Pizza Hut breath."

"Stop!" I cry. "There will definitely not be any kissing."

Mattie laughs. "That's what you think!" she says, hanging up.

Kissing? A maybe-date I can handle, but kissing is something else altogether. Okay, *now* I'm nervous. If my alarm clock is right, it is six-thirty. It takes fifteen minutes to walk to Pizza Hut. If I leave now, I'll have another fifteen minutes to wait. I don't want to be too early, but if I stay here I'll keep re-checking my hair and re-thinking my outfit. I'll go crazy.

"That shirt looks better on you than it ever did on me."

"Mom!"

My mother leans in the doorway, sipping from a blue energy drink and looking wistful. She's just come back from the gym, her cheeks all rosy and her hair all wispy. She could be in a workout video.

"Thanks," I say, pulling the shirt down for the one hundredth time.

"I had too much going on up here to really pull it off," she says, gesturing at her chest.

"*Mom!*"

"But it looks cute as a button on you."

"Thanks," I say, glancing at the alarm clock. It is now six-thirty-five. "I should probably go."

"Don't let me keep you," Mom says. "Have fun, baby."

"You, too," I say, feeling guilty for lying about my (maybe) date.

I bet some girls — girls like Mattie — can't wait to come home and tell their moms all about their (maybe) dates. Part of me wants to do the same thing, but another part of me hesitates. She's bound to make a big deal out of it, and I'm not sure I want to talk about it yet. Plus how am I supposed to explain how I feel about Michael when I can barely wrap my head around the whole situation myself? Then there's the Doug factor. If I tell her about Michael, does that mean I have to listen to her stories about Doug? Because I can't handle any more gushing about Doug's business or his do-it-yourself projects or his silly, brainless excuse of a dog. Don't ask, don't tell; at the moment, this seems like the best philosophy.

Mom doesn't seem to pick up on any of this, thank goodness. She smiles and says, "Don't worry about me, I'm a big girl."

But I do worry. In the back of my mind, I'm always worrying about her. What if she's taking on too much? What if she isn't getting enough rest? She looks healthy now, and according to the doctors she's making amazing progress. But until they say the word remission, I think I'll always worry a little bit. It's like the birthmark on my hip, the one shaped like a half moon; it's something people rarely see, something I can cover up easily, but it's there, permanently.

* * *

When I arrive at Pizza Hut, with exactly five minutes to spare, there is a wait for a table. I glance around the dining room but all I see are families and groups of teenagers, stuffing their faces with cheesy, gooey pizza that makes my stomach grumble. Michael is nowhere to be seen.

"Hot date?" the hostess asks. She's wearing too much makeup and looks miserable. I'd be miserable too if I had to wear that Pizza Hut visor all night.

"No," I say coldly. "I'm just looking for my friend."

The hostess smirks, cracking the heavy layer of foundation on her cheeks. "This friend, is he a boy?" she asks.

"Yes," I admit.

"A boy*friend*?"

"He is a boy who happens to be my friend," I say, and then I sit on the red plastic couch, next to a couple who are also waiting. I pretend to be interested in the paper someone left behind. The hostess laughs and disappears into the kitchen, probably to reapply the lip gloss that's all over her teeth.

I try not to look at the big clock above the hostess station. Six-fifty-eight. Seven o'clock. Seven-oh-five. How much time has to go by before someone is officially late?

The awful hostess comes back with even shinier and pinker lips. She shows the couple sitting next to me to their table. When she returns, she leans across the counter and smirks at me again. "Maybe you've been stood up." I ignore her. She speaks up again, this time a little louder. "That's pretty grim, to be stood up at a Pizza Hut."

"It can't be worse than working at a Pizza Hut," I shoot back.

The hostess narrows her eyes until there are only thick black smudges of eyeliner where her eyes should be. Honestly, it looks like she applied it with a crayon. She looks like she's getting ready to say something when the door opens. We both look over. Michael rushes in, looking sheepish.

He's wearing real pants (no jeans! no sweatpants!) and a short-sleeved, button-down shirt that is coming untucked on one side. He smiles at me and smoothes his hair, which has been parted on the side and swept forward, like he's on the cover of *Teen People*. His hair isn't quite long enough to pull it off; thick cowlicks keep curling back on themselves. That's when I know for sure: this is a date.

The hostess looks from Michael to me. "Is this him?" she says.

I stand a little taller. "Yes, this is my *friend*," I confirm.

"Hi, Clarissa! Have you been waiting long?"

"Not really," I lie.

The hostess snorts. "This way," she says curtly.

Why do dates have to be held in public places? I feel like everyone is watching us make our way to the table. A woman I don't even know looks up from wiping the pizza sauce off her kid's face and smiles at me. Can she tell we're on a date just by looking at us? She doesn't know that I generally avoid skirts and that Michael's hair generally falls in neat waves on either side of a middle part. I fiddle with the edge of my Hufflepuff shirt, the one familiar thing in this whole bizarre situation.

"Here you are, *kids*," the hostess says, taking extra pleasure in calling us kids.

I glare at her but Michael doesn't seem to notice. "Thanks," he says, taking a menu. "Oh, hey, look — they have double-stuffed crust upside-down pizza!"

The hostess wiggles her overplucked eyebrows at me. "Have fun," she says, sauntering back to the hostess station.

Even though I'm glad that she's gone, now I am alone with Michael. Usually there is someone else around, someone chatty, like Mattie. Now I'm going to have to do all the talking myself. Luckily Michael is busy studying the menu. I do the same.

"Everything looks good," Michael says. "What are you going to get?"

"Probably just pizza," I admit. "I don't need anything too fancy."

"The pasta is really good here," Michael says. "Maybe we could get one of the combos and split it." I never considered ordering pasta at Pizza Hut. It's not called pasta hut, after all. But tonight is all about trying new things.

"It also comes with a salad and a pitcher of pop," Michael reads. "What kind of pop do you like?"

"Orange," I reply.

Michael smiles. "Me, too. Salad?"

"Caesar."

"Me, too."

Now I'm smiling.

The waitress is probably about the same age as the hostess but she is much nicer. "How are you guys doing tonight?" she asks. "What brings you to the Hut?"

"Actually, we won a badminton tournament," Michael says, beaming at me.

My cheeks are beginning to hurt from all the smiling, but I can't seem to stop.

"No way!" says the waitress. "Well, good for you. I'm terrible at badminton." It is easy to see how she's moved up in the ranks and the surly hostess has not. "Have you had a chance to look at the menus?"

"I think we've decided," I say, and Michael nods.

The waitress retrieves a pencil from behind her ear and flips to a fresh page on her waitress pad. "Well, what do champions like to eat?"

"We'll have the pasta and pizza combo," I say.

"You know you get salad and a pitcher of pop with that, right?" the waitress asks.

"We'll have the Caesar salad —" I begin.

"— and orange pop," Michael finishes.

"Good stuff," says the waitress. "And since you're big-time badminton champs and all, how about I throw in some cheesy garlic bread, on the house?"

"Thanks!" says Michael.

"Any time. My name is Melanie if you guys need anything."

Melanie leaves and Michael and I grin at each other for a while. I can't think of anything to say, my mind is completely blank. All I can think about is how at first I didn't really like his new hair but now it's growing on me. It makes him look older. This is not the sort of thing you say to a boy.

The silence is starting to feel awkward. Finally Michael says, "You look nice."

"Thanks," I reply. "So do you. I like your hair."

I can't believe I said that. Apparently, neither can Michael. He blushes and immediately smoothes it to one side. "You noticed?"

"Of course I noticed. I live with a hair stylist."

"Oh, right. How is your mom?" Michael asks.

"Good, I mean, she's doing better. She's done chemo and everything. For the moment, anyway."

Michael nods but doesn't say anything more. I'm relieved. Cancer is not date-appropriate conversation. Melanie brings us the cheesy garlic bread. I'm not sure, but it looks like she got them to put extra cheese on it. You can barely see the bread underneath all that bubbly goodness. Michael and I tuck in and I'm excused from making conversation yet again. This must be why people go to restaurants for dates; you spend half the time eating instead of talking.

"Once my little brother ate an entire basket of cheesy garlic bread by himself," Michael says.

"How old was he?" I ask.

"Five. He puked it all up like an hour later."

"Gross," I say, trying not to picture it. "Do you just have the one brother?" I ask.

Michael shakes his head. "Nope, I have three: Theo, David, and Solly."

"Wow, that's a lot of boys," I say aloud. To myself I think, poor Mrs. Greenblat.

"It can get pretty crazy at our house sometimes," Michael admits. "Especially with the dog, Rambo."

"Is he as crazy as he sounds?" I ask.

Michael grins. "Worse."

I'm thinking that Michael's living situation sounds like my worst nightmare when Melanie arrives with the biggest bowl of Caesar salad I've ever seen.

"Parmesan cheese?" she asks.

Michael and I answer at once. "Yes, please."

Melanie whistles. "I can see why you two made such a good team. I wouldn't want to meet you guys on the badminton court."

"It was all Clarissa, really," Michael says graciously. "She's the one with the plan."

Melanie smiles at me and gives me a little wink. Thankfully Michael doesn't seem to notice. He's too busy shovelling forkfuls of lettuce dripping in Caesar salad dressing into his mouth.

Now, I'm not Mattie and I think it's silly to eat teeny tiny amounts of food in front of boys, but all that cheesy garlic bread and salad is starting to fill me up. We haven't even reached the main course yet. I put my utensils down and inch my chair away from the table.

"This is pretty great," I say. "It's like a free four-course meal."

"Don't forget dessert," Michael adds.

"I completely forgot about dessert!" I say. "I'm never going to have enough room."

"I bet I can guess what you put on your sundae," Michael boasts.

"Oh, really?"

"Really."

"Okay, guess."

"Well, I know you really like chocolate, so chocolate sauce, chocolate chips, and Smarties for sure. Right?"

"Yes," I admit reluctantly. "But everyone likes chocolate. What else?"

"Well, even though I think it's totally gross to mix them with chocolate sauce, Nerds."

I have to keep my jaw from dropping open.

"Well? Am I right?" Michael asks.

"How did you know that?" I ask.

Michael shrugs. "Easy, you always get Nerds every time you go to the 7-Eleven. They're your favourite candy."

"But how do you know that?" I press.

Michael looks right at me. "Because I like you."

At first I'm not sure if I've heard him correctly, but he looks down at his food and keeps pushing a crouton around on his plate like it's a matter of life or death. I open my mouth to speak a few times, but what comes out is all gar-bled and sounds something like this: "Because you — Oh, okay. Good."

Michael looks up hopefully. "Good?" he repeats.

I feel like I've been backed into a corner. It is good, right? I like that Michael likes me, and even though I'd never admit it, I kind of sort of like him, too. But now that it's out there, what happens next? Do we start hanging out together, just the two of us? Do I have to start calling him my boyfriend? I don't think I could do that. It's probably best to be as vague as possible.

"Yeah, good," I confirm.

Michael looks confused, and then relieved, and then Melanie arrives with the pizza. Thank goodness.

"Here you are, guys," she says. "I'll be right back with your pasta. You saved room, right?"

"Barely," I say weakly, still stunned from Michael's confession. I grab a slice and busy myself with eating once again.

"You're lucky you got a table when you did," Melanie says. "It's hopping in here tonight. Just look at that line."

Michael and I look over at the group of people waiting around on the plastic couches near the door — an elderly couple; a family with a bunch of kids; and right in front, waiting to be seated, is my mother and Doug.

"Hey, isn't that —"

"Yes, yes it is." I put my half-eaten slice of pizza on my plate and slink down in my chair. My face is hot and I feel physically sick.

"Who is she with?" Michael asks.

"Doug," I say, without offering any other explanation.

"Is that her boyfriend or something?"

I put my head into my hands and moan.

Michael looks at me and frowns. "You don't look so good," he says.

"I think I ate too much," I lie, or maybe it's the truth. My stomach is definitely upset.

"Are you going to puke?" Michael asks, looking a little concerned but mostly grossed out. "Maybe you should go to the bathroom."

Sneaking away to the bathroom is exactly what I want to do. Unfortunately I'd have to walk right by the lineup to get there. No thanks. Instead, I slink down a little lower in my seat and hope that they don't see me. Maybe they'll be too lovey-dovey to notice anyone else. Then the couple next to us waves down Melanie and asks for the cheque.

"Sure thing," she says, clearing their dishes. "Hey, Krista," she calls over her shoulder. The surly hostess looks over at her. "Table for two, coming right up."

And that's how I end up on a double date with my mother.

Four

The tables at Pizza Hut are crammed in to accommodate as many customers as possible, so even though Mom and Doug are technically at a separate table, we might as well be sitting together. The ten seconds it takes for Melanie to lead my mom and Doug to the table beside us feels like the longest ten seconds in my life. Doug does the world's biggest double take before raising his big paw of a hand to wave while my mother just smiles.

"Well, look who we've got here," Doug says.

"Mattie, how you've changed," Mom says coolly, looking from Michael to me.

Michael laughs nervously. "Hi, Miss Delaney, do you remember me? I'm —"

"Michael Greenblat, yes I remember. We met at my surprise welcome home party. It's very good to see you again."

Doug offers Michael a meaty hand. "Doug Armstrong, nice to meet you, son."

Michael shakes Doug's hand. "Michael Greenblat, um, sir."

Doug slaps him on the shoulder and practically howls with laughter. People crane their necks to see what all the fuss is about. I don't know what it is about my mother and loud people. Between Doug and Denise, there can't be a louder person in the whole town.

"You don't mind if we take this table, do you Clarissa?" Mom asks me pointedly.

"No," I manage to say. "Of course not."

Melanie has been watching the whole disaster with a curious smile on her face. "Wait," she says, "how do you all know each other?"

Mom drapes an arm around my shoulders. The squeeze she gives them feels a little tighter than usual. "Clarissa here is my daughter," she explains.

"Ohh . . ." Melanie looks both relieved and a little guilty. As my mom turns to take her seat, Melanie steals a glance at me and mouths "sorry." Yeah, you and me both, Melanie.

"What brings you kids to the Hut?" Doug asks, reaching around Michael and helping himself to a slice of our pizza. Somehow he manages to eat the whole thing in less than three bites.

Michael looks at me funny. "Didn't Clarissa tell you?" he says, looking from me to my mom to Doug and back at me again. I ignore the pain in my stomach and the burning in my cheeks by busying myself with a generous helping of pasta.

"Tell us what?" Doug asks, eyeing the pizza but managing to restrain himself from grabbing another slice.

"We won gift certificates in a badminton tournament," Michael says.

"Oh, yes, I remember now," Mom says. Under the table, her foot presses lightly into the back of my leg. I flash her a grateful smile, but she pretends not to notice.

"No kidding?" Doug is truly impressed. "I had no idea you were such an athlete, Clarissa."

"It's just badminton," I mumble through a mouthful of spaghetti. "Besides, Michael got all the hard shots."

"You had all those sneak attacks," Michael protests. "And you were the one with the strategies."

"This calls for a toast," says Doug. He reaches for his water glass and holds it in the air. Mom and Michael follow suit. Reluctantly, I hold up my own glass of pop. "To Michael and Clarissa, badminton champs."

We clink our plastic glasses and all take a sip of our respective beverages. Everyone at the table behind us has turned around to watch. Doug nudges the mom with a toddler in her lap. The kid's face is smeared with tomato sauce. "Did you know you're sitting near two badminton champs?"

She smiles, charmed, and shakes her head. "No, I did not. Congratulations," she says. The baby thrusts his fist at Doug, who makes a shocked face and then pretends to eat the baby's fingers. Everyone laughs, but no one is more delighted than the baby. Except for my own mother, who is openly staring at Doug with a goofy look on her face. Barf.

"So is this badminton talent hereditary?" Doug asks me, looking at my mother. "Just one more thing that Annie Delaney is good at?"

"Oh, cut it out," Mom says, but she smiles like she doesn't mean it.

"I don't know," I answer honestly. "I've never seen her play."

Doug leans forward, both elbows on the table, and looks my mom straight in the eye. "Well then I, Douglas Armstrong, challenge you, Annette Delaney, to a badminton match. My gym, you name the date. Loser has to make the winner a candlelight dinner."

Mom laughs, offers her hand, and the two of them shake. "Deal," she says.

And so for the rest of the evening, Michael and I have dinner with Mom and Doug. I guess it's not all bad. The one thing that's nice about sharing a table is that now there are more people to talk with; it's not just me and Michael struggling to carry on a conversation. Michael seems to really like Doug. They talk about basketball and Doug's gym and some video game I've never heard of.

Somehow we make it through the pizza and the dessert course and it's finally time to leave.

"Are you walking home?" Mom asks, glancing out the window at the dusk that has fallen while we ate.

"Yes," I say, thinking that no, I was actually walking to Mattie's house. But I can't admit that without letting Michael know and reminding my mother that I was supposed to be at Mattie's all along.

"I'll walk her home, Miss Delaney," Michael pipes up.

"Good man," says Doug.

"Have a good night you two," Mom says, her eyes twinkling.

"Thanks, Miss Delaney."

Mom reaches out and squeezes Michael's hand. "Call me Annie, sweetheart."

"Thanks, Annie. It was nice to see you again."

"You, too. And, Michael, you stop by after school sometime and I'll give you a trim. I like what you've got going on there," she says, pointing at the shock of hair that keeps falling over one eye. "Very hip, very now."

"Okay, cool," says Michael.

Doug raises his fist and bumps knuckles with Michael. "See you around."

Michael hands over the gift certificates and we are out of there.

Kiss

"Doug seems nice," Michael says.

We're walking back to my place. I'm careful to keep my hands in my pockets, just in case Michael gets any crazy ideas about holding hands. I will myself not to shiver; it's much colder out now than when I left and I forgot my jacket at home. I'm worried that if I look too cold Michael will offer me his, or worse, try to put his arm around my shoulders.

"I guess," I say.

"How long have they been dating?" Michael asks.

"They're not dating," I say sharply.

"Oh. It seemed like they were."

"If you were on a date, would you sit with your kid and her badminton partner?" Michael looks hurt. I'm not sure if it's because I insinuated that he wasn't cool enough to warrant Doug's attention or because I called him my badminton partner and not my date. I back-pedal a little. "It's too early to really say if they're dating or not," I mutter.

Michael nods, like he understands. "That must be weird, your mom dating," he says. "I can barely stand it when my parents get all lovey-dovey, and they've been kissing in front of me my whole life."

I almost stop walking. "You think they kiss?"

"Who?"

"My mom and Doug!"

Michael looks at me like I've been living under a rock. "Well, probably. They're adults. Everybody kisses."

Now we've stopped walking. Is it my imagination, or is Michael standing a little closer? He clears his throat and his eyes get all shifty. One second they're looking at me, the next they're landing on my mouth, then over my shoulder. I feel cold and hot all at once. I rub my arms to make the feeling go away and start to walk — a little faster now. "Well, not in front of me they don't."

Michael hurries to catch up. We walk the rest of the way home in silence. Finally we're at the house. "Here we are!" I say brightly. I sound fake, even to myself. I just want to get in the door and away from any possible kissing. My heart is banging around in my chest so loudly it's a miracle that Michael hasn't heard it. It makes my hands shake as I fumble for my key.

"Thanks for walking me," I say.

Michael shrugs. "No problem." He smiles and takes a step toward me. "I had a nice time."

"Me, too." After a second I add, "I should probably head in."

Michael nods, but makes no move to leave. "Okay."

"I'd invite you in, but my mom probably wouldn't like it."

"That's okay. . . . You're a really good badminton player, Clarissa." Before I can say anything he goes on, "And you're really smart, too."

"I'm not, really. I can think of ten people in our class alone who are smarter."

"I can't," Michael says. He takes another step toward me. He is now standing in the circle of yellow light cast by the porch lamp.

"You're really good, too," I say lamely, fumbling for the doorknob. "At school and badminton." I glance wildly at Benji's house, to see if maybe he's sitting in the window, but it's completely dark. Probably out with his theatre friends at karaoke or something. I feel abandoned. Michael closes the gap between us, one shuffley step at a time.

"See you Monday!" I manage to turn the key and shove the door open with my shoulder in one smooth motion. I don't even turn around to wave. Inside, I lean against the door until I'm sure that Michael has left. I close my eyes and take deep calming breaths through my nose until my heart stops hammering against my chest. For some reason, tears form at the corners of my eyes. I sniff them back, furiously. I don't know why I'm so upset. The thought of kissing makes my head spin and my palms clammy. But the thought of Michael walking home all dejected makes me feel even worse.

What's wrong with me? If I had been Mattie or any other girl in the class I would probably be skipping off to call my best friend to tell her all about my magical first kiss with Michael. Instead, here I am, snivelling away in the dark, because I'm too chicken. It's not that I don't want to kiss him *ever*, I just don't want to kiss him right now or in the immediate future. Somehow I doubt that will make Michael feel better. Mattie's right, I am abnormal. Michael deserves someone else. Someone who, at the very least, would be happy to kiss him.

***

Later, at Mattie's, drinking hot chocolate made with real milk and mini-marshmallows, I tell her the whole story — except for the part about me crying in the dark.

"Do you think I'm an idiot?" I ask, fully expecting her to yell at me about how I totally blew the perfect moment.

"No," she says. "You're a romantic. You might not think you are, but I can tell. You want your first kiss to be the right person at the right time."

I consider this for a moment before asking, "What if it was the right person at the right time and I totally ruined it?"

"No," Mattie says thoughtfully. "Right person, wrong time. I totally believe that you and Michael are destined to be together. You're just not ready. And that doesn't make you a baby," she adds quickly. "It makes you smart."

I feel warm and fuzzy, and not just from the hot chocolate. "Michael said I was smart," I remember.

Mattie rolls her eyes. "That's because you are."

"So are you. You're incredibly wise and you make the best hot chocolate I've ever had."

Mattie giggles. "You know, it's probably a good thing you didn't kiss tonight."

"Why?" I ask.

"Because you must have had terrible pizza breath." I throw a marshmallow at her head but at the last second she bobs up and catches it in her mouth. We both burst out laughing.

"Nice reflexes," I say. "Too bad you couldn't use them in badminton."

Mattie gasps and for a split second I worry that maybe it was too soon for that kind of comment, but she grins, grabs a handful of marshmallows, and starts launching a counterattack. "Take it back!" she laughs.

"Never!" I cry, and we continue throwing marshmallows at each other until Cheryl comes into the kitchen and tells us to keep it down.

Trim

I make it through breakfast and most of the morning without having to revisit the double date debacle with my mom, until she knocks on my bedroom door and says, "Are you still in your pyjamas?" Followed immediately by, "It's time for a cut."

I run my hands as best as I can through the tangled mess that sticks out from my head in all directions. "I like it this length."

"A trim, then."

To the untrained ear my mother's voice seems light, but I can hear the iron in it. It's no use. I'm caught. "Okay," I agree, and follow her downstairs to the Hair Emporium.

Normally, Mom would flip on the radio and hum along (off key) as she sets up her arsenal, but today she gets right down to business. I climb into the chair. The leather squeaks under my thighs. It's the only sound in the otherwise creepily silent salon. Mom runs her fingers through the length of my hair — a little forcefully, if you ask me — barking instructions. "Tilt your head. Now to the left. Look straight ahead. Hmmm . . ."

I so desperately want to make conversation about something, anything, but the only thing I can think about is the double date, which is exactly what I'm trying to avoid, and so I don't say a word, even as Mom spritzes my face instead of my hair and digs the comb into my scalp. There is nothing worse than a silent salon. Mom says it's a sign of mistrust between the stylist and her client.

I clear my throat about a million times, but the only thing I manage to get out is, "Not too much off."

"Don't worry," Mom says breezily, "you're in good hands." She fans the apron around me and snaps it tightly around my neck. The thing about getting your hair cut is there's nowhere to go. You're trapped in the chair at the mercy of a woman with scissors. And sometimes a razor. "So. How is Mattie?"

"Fine. We had hot chocolate."

"When was this?" Mom asks.

"Last night."

"What time last night? Because I seem to recall seeing you at Pizza Hut around seven-thirty."

Well what do you say to that? "I guess it was closer to eight-thirty."

"So this is after you went to Pizza Hut . . ." Mom presses.

"Yes."

". . . with Michael . . ."

"Yes."

". . . who is your badminton partner."

"Yes."

"Interesting." Mom cuts furiously. I am worried about the amount of hair that is piling up on the floor at my feet. "Aren't you going to ask me how *my* night was?" she asks.

"How was your night?" I say obediently.

Mom smiles, but it's a little too maniacal to put me at

ease. "Wonderful. I had a lovely time with Doug, who is just as sweet as pie. We had dinner and saw a movie. Thank you for asking."

I squirm in my seat. It's hot under this apron. "So, you're dating? For real?"

Mom stops cutting and looks at me in the mirror. "Yes. We're dating. For real. Are you dating?"

"No!"

Mom narrows her eyes. "Are you sure? Because it certainly looked like you were on a date."

"It wasn't a date. We had to use up those gift certificates, otherwise they'd go to waste. You can't *not* use gift certificates . . ." I trail off, painfully aware of how lame I sound.

"Will there be more dates?" Mom asks.

I shrug. "Maybe. No. I don't know. It's not like you and Doug."

"What's that supposed to mean?"

"I mean I'm not going to spend all my time talking to him or about him or bonding with his stupid dog."

Mom puts both hands on the chair and turns it so we're face to face. "What is wrong with you? So you get to go gallivanting with a boy I barely know and I can't spend a few hours with Doug, who has been nothing but kind to you? Don't I get to be happy, too?" she asks.

"So I make you unhappy?"

"Clarissa, don't do this. You're twisting my words. Of course I'm happy with you. Maybe right now I'm not ecstatic with your behaviour, but I've never been anything but thrilled about you. But I am an adult, and I get to go on dates and have fun and fall in love if I want to."

"Fall in love?" I repeat.

"Yes, fall in love. Haven't I earned that?"

"Yes," I say.

"Good. Then we agree." For a second I think that's it and she'll go back to being the stylist and I'll go back to being the client and in ten minutes I can run as far away from this salon as possible. But she continues. "Honestly, the way you've been behaving you'd think you were the most hard done by kid in the world. Have I ever, to your recollection, brought a man home for dinner?"

"No."

"Or gone out on a real, bona-fide date?"

"No."

"Exactly. You know, there are some single women out there who never let their kids get in the way of their love lives. I could have had a whole string of men, but I didn't. That's not me. This is my life, you and this salon, and that's fine with me. But then someone like Doug comes along and you think, maybe there could be something more, you know?"

I don't know. This isn't really the kind of conversation I want to have with my mother. I don't like to hear how the salon and I are suddenly not enough for her. A wild wave of rage like I haven't felt in ages washes over me and I have to grip the sides of the chair to stay calm. I'm not mad at her, not really; I'm mad at the universe or God or whatever supposedly greater power it was that poisoned my mom's body with cancer and wrecked everything. Before the cancer, we never fought like this. Before the cancer, the salon and I were enough for her, there was no Doug. So what if the surgery is done and the chemo is over and her hair is growing back; here we are, a year later, and cancer is still ruining our lives.

"Like you and Michael. What's going on there?" my

mom continues. "I didn't even know you played badminton. How do you think it feels to learn about your daughter winning a badminton championship in front of someone else? I'll tell you how I felt: I felt like a bad mother."

"You're not a bad mother."

"But I felt like one."

"I'm sorry."

Mom stops cutting and sighs, looking at me in the mirror. "What happened to us?" she asks. "We used to tell each other things."

I shrug. I don't know what happened. Somewhere along the line, some things became too hard to say out loud. It's easier to not say anything at all.

Mom tucks a damp strand of hair behind my ear. "I want us to be able to tell each other things again," she says. "Don't you?"

I shrug. I start to say I guess, but the look on my mother's face is so heartbreaking that I change my mind and say as firmly as I can, "Yes, I do."

She smiles and loosens the waves of my hair with her fingers. "There. I feel better. Don't you?"

"Yes," I lie.

The Benj

"What's that noise?" Mom asks, glancing at one of the windows in the salon. Loud, obnoxious laughter filters through the screen and disrupts the peace and quiet of the Hair Emporium. Ambiance is everything to my mom. She frowns slightly and turns the volume on the radio up a notch.

Dolly, one of her oldest and most loyal clients, sniffs in distaste. "Teenagers," she says, rolling her eyes.

I clear my throat. I may not be loud and obnoxious, but I am still technically a teenager and I take offense to that eye roll.

"Sorry, Clarissa," Dolly apologizes. "I can't imagine *you* making such a fuss."

"That's because I wouldn't," I say.

"That's my girl, thirteen going on sixty-five," Mom says. She smiles and I smile back. Ever since my impromptu haircut we've been very polite with each other.

Dolly wags her finger at my mom. "Nothing wrong with sixty-five," she scolds.

"Oh, Dolly, you don't look a day over fifty," Mom says, and the two of them laugh. She looks back at the window. "I may be wrong, but it sounds like it's coming from Benji's place."

"No, not Benjamin, he's such a sweet boy," Dolly protests. "Speaking of boys, I hear you found yourself a man, Annie."

"A girl can't keep a secret in this town," Mom says, grinning slyly.

"I'll go check on that noise," I offer, before she can delve into all the details. But neither Mom nor Dolly look over from their conversation. I hop up from my perch at the hair dryer where I've been flipping through an old magazine looking for alcohol ads for my advertising project. It's not due for two weeks, but without Benji to entertain me I've been disturbingly productive where schoolwork is concerned.

Upstairs, I pause in the living room and peer out the curtains in the bay window. Sure enough, Benji and his theatre friends are draped all over his front porch, chatting. One of them, a girl with a long, thick braid reaching almost to her waist, sits cross-legged on the grass, occasionally stretching an arm over her head. She is clearly a dancer. A blonde girl with dark glasses keeps taking her hair down and then rearranging it in various ponytails, almost like she has a tic. Either that or the boy she's talking to makes her nervous. He looks like he spends a lot of time at the gym, but he has unfortunate hair that looks like it would be curly if he would just let it grow a little bit. Instead, it sticks out all over his head in a dense fuzzy mess, like a Brillo pad. All three of them look like they're in high school; I don't recognize any of them from Ferndale.

Benji sits next to Charity, she of the siren-red locks and professional resumé. The other three keep trying to engage Benji and Charity in conversation. I can hear them from my secret post by the window. Each one is louder than the next.

"I don't like the new choreographer either," the dancer says, pulling her feet in to touch her thighs. She is incredibly flexible. "She's trying too hard. I mean, it's community theatre, half the cast has never been to a dance class before. It took the Munchkins a half-hour to get the box step down pat, how does she expect them to master a real jazz combination?"

Glasses snorts and does an impression of someone, a Munchkin I guess, flailing her arms and falling all over the porch steps. The group bursts into laughter. They grab their stomachs or slap the porch and wipe tears from their eyes. I've never seen a group of people laugh so hard in my life. It doesn't seem real, it's like they're acting all the time. I'm exhausted just watching them. Benji wraps his arms around his legs and giggles madly into his knees.

I feel weird listening to them, like I'm spying. I know I should go over and say hello but I can't shake the feeling that maybe Benji doesn't want me there. If he did, wouldn't he have invited me over when he got home from rehearsal? No. I'm being ridiculous. I can't sit here hiding behind the curtain all day. Benji is my best friend, why shouldn't I go over and say hello?

I slip out the back door. Benji looks over as the screen door slams behind me. His face lights up and the knots in my stomach melt away. "Clarissa!" he exclaims. He sounds genuinely happy to see me.

"Hey," I say, disguising my nerves with a casual tone and praying that no one saw me hiding behind the curtains in the bay window.

The theatre kids smile at me and practically fall all over each other to shake my hand and introduce themselves. Glasses turns out to be Mika, the dancer is Katie, and the boy goes by Beckett.

"Beckett?" I repeat.

The boy shrugs. "Yeah, I know, it's weird. My mom named me after this playwright no one's ever heard of."

"Excuse me," Mika interrupts, "but Samuel Beckett is a revolutionary playwright. It's not like he's someone obscure, like Wycherly or Albee."

Charity and Katie laugh. Beckett rolls his eyes.

"Can you imagine if your mom named you Albee?" Katie says.

"Okay, so no one but hardcore drama students like you dorks has ever heard of him," Beckett says.

"Beckett's mom teaches drama at the high school," Charity says. "She also directs all the major Gaslight Community Players shows."

I guess this explains the Beckett thing.

"Not all of them," Beckett protests.

"All of the good ones," Mika says. "We are seriously lucky to have her." I wonder who Mika is more in love with, Beckett or his director mother.

"Are you an actor, too?" Katie asks me.

"Sort of," I say.

"How come you didn't audition for *The Wizard*?" Mika asks, slipping the elastic out of her hair again.

"I did."

An awkward silence settles over the group. "I'm not really into musicals," I say quickly. "I'm not much of a singer."

"Don't worry, Clarissa," Charity says. "Actors face tons of rejection."

All of a sudden the whole group is talking at once, telling me about the shows they didn't make, and all the horrible auditions they've had. They compete to see who had the worst audition or the most rejections. Instead of making me feel better, it makes me feel worse. How can my one

123

measly rejection compare to their endless audition horror stories? It's just one more thing I don't have in common with them.

Suddenly Mika jumps into the conversation, squealing, "Oh my God, did you see what Dopey was wearing today?"

"Dopey?" I repeat.

"The ASM," Charity says, as if that's supposed to clarify things.

"Assistant stage manager," Benji explains.

"Right, right, sorry, I forget that people don't know what that means," Charity apologizes. She doesn't seem all that sorry to me. "We call him Dopey because his ears stick straight out, like Dopey from *Snow White and the Seven Dwarfs*, you know, the Disney one?" She must have seen my face, because she adds quickly, "We don't call him that to his face, we're not horrible people."

"Anyway," Mika says, looking directly at me, "Dopey is, like, the king of AV at school and he is madly in love with Charity."

"He is not," Charity protests, but the group all cries out in agreement with Mika.

"He's like a sad, lovesick puppy," Katie says.

"Yeah, a puppy who has been hit by three Cupid tranquilizer darts," Beckett adds.

"ANYWAY, so today he shows up wearing his *Les Mis* t-shirt from, like, four years ago. How sad is that? I don't even know where mine is."

When it becomes clear that no one is going to explain to me what a *Les Mis* t-shirt is and why it's so hysterically funny, I get up to leave.

"Where are you going?" Benji asks.

"I have stuff to do," I say.

"What kind of stuff?" Charity asks.

I shrug. "Oh, homework, chores, that kind of stuff." Benji frowns and I look away, avoiding his gaze. He knows I never do chores or homework on weekends if I can help it.

Charity pats the step beside her. "Can't it wait? We want to get to know you. The Benj is always going on about you."

The Benj? What kind of a nickname is that? Still, hope, like a single birthday candle, flickers in my chest. If Benji talks about me to these loud, funny, and interesting people, he can't have totally forgotten me. But even though I'm tempted, it doesn't feel right to stay and hang out with them. I don't know any of the people they know, and I don't understand any of their inside jokes. I'm not a part of their crowd. To them, I'm just another audience member.

"Maybe another time," I say. "It was nice meeting you."

Inside, I go down to the basement and turn the TV on as loud as I can without Mom hollering at me to turn it down. That way, I don't have to hear the laughter coming from Benji's yard.

Envy

Benji's new theatre friends have been showering him with soundtracks from all kinds of musicals I've never heard of. He plays them for me when I go over to visit him. "Listen to this song, isn't it amazing?"

After listening to *Rent*, *Spring Awakening*, and *Les Misérables* from beginning to end, I think it's safe to say that as much as I love acting, musical theatre is not my thing. *Hairspray* was pretty funny, though.

There are so many things that are going on in my life that Benji doesn't know about. I can't remember a time when this was the case. It's always been the two of us. Now I have to repeat conversations that he missed, or listen to him describe people I've never met. It makes me think about what Mom said — that in high school everything changes. It's starting to feel true already. But what if I don't want it to be true?

"You should come to one of our SAPS," Benji says.

"What's that?"

"It stands for Saturday After Practice Shindigs — I told you about them last week. It's when we get together after rehearsal to just hang out."

"What do you do?"

"All kinds of things, sometimes we go out to dinner, or

go to someone's house and watch movies and play improv games and stuff."

"I don't know, it sounds like it's just for cast members."

"Not at all!" Benji insists. "People bring friends all the time. Last week we played musical charades. Charity and I won. You could be on our team."

"No, thanks. I'd rather watch movies with Denise." I admit that was a bit low. That is generally the kind of comment I reserve for people who get on my nerves and Benji knows it, only he's never been on the receiving end before.

In the old days, before he became an actor and hung out with his actor friends, Benji would've frowned, I would've apologized right away, he'd forgive me and that would be that. But this Benji, or should I say, The Benj, just looks me straight in the eye and says, "Fine. But one of these days I'm just going to stop asking you."

Well, good. That's fine with me. Who wants to hang out with a bunch of drama queens anyway?

***

Mattie is no help where the Benji issue is concerned. The one time I open up and tell her I've been missing him, she immediately jumps to conclusions. "Now don't get mad, but are you sure you're not jealous because secretly you have feelings for Benji?"

"No! Why does everyone keep asking me that? I am not in love with Benji, he is my best friend! Can't a girl be friends with a boy without it being all about love?"

"Okay, okay, I just wanted to check!"

If I had a dollar for every time someone asked me if Benji was my boyfriend, I'd be a zillionaire by now. Of course I love Benji, but I love him the way you love your best friend, or a brother. I'd jump in front of a bus for him but that doesn't mean I'm *in* love with him. I don't think about kissing him or wonder what it would feel like to have his arm around my shoulders.

The way I feel about Michael is totally different. With Michael, it's all butterflies and tingling and curiosity, but Benji is so familiar he's like a part of me, like a leg, or my nose. The way I feel about Benji is deeper than how I feel about Michael. Without him, I wouldn't feel like me. Maybe it should be the other way around; shouldn't I be in love with the person I care the most about? I don't get love. Maybe no one does. Maybe that's why there are so many songs and books devoted to it. It makes me feel a little better knowing it's not just me, that the whole world is trying to figure it out.

Like, or
Like-Like?

Now that Mattie and I are completely over the Josh fiasco, I have someone to talk to about the Michael situation. Benji knows the basics, but I haven't told him everything. It's weird to talk to a boy about another boy, even if one of those boys is Benji, who I consider a friend first, boy second. A part of me is keeping the I Like You confession to myself because Benji has this whole other secret life with his stupid play, and now I have this secret about Michael. Now we both have things in our lives that the other person isn't involved in.

"What it all comes down to is the fact that he actually said the words 'I like you,' right?" Mattie asks.

"Yes," I confirm, blushing at the memory. "Those were his exact words."

"And you said what?"

"I said 'that's good,'" I admit.

Mattie sighs. "*That's good*? Poor Michael. He's probably confused."

The bell jangles and both of us look over to see who has walked into the arcade. Normally I would never set foot in an arcade, but Mattie heard that Declan James, her latest crush, is a huge arcade and video game nut. That alone is enough to turn me off, but Mattie doesn't seem to mind. So here we are. Luckily the arcade has a pretty good selection of candy.

When I pointed out that video game prowess doesn't seem like much of a skill, Mattie said, "Good hand-eye coordination is important. Maybe he'll be a surgeon." Doubtful. I think you have to be good at school to become a doctor and the only thing Declan has going for him is that apparently he can beat some video game I've never even heard of in two hours. That and he is pretty cute. Otherwise he's just as lame as Josh, but with nicer skin.

The customer heads over to Dance Dance Revolution and deposits a handful of change into the machine. Definitely not Declan.

"Mattie, what's the big deal with Declan anyway?"

Mattie shrugs. "He's cute. Don't you think he's cute?"

"I guess, but have you ever talked to him? Has he ever said one nice thing to you?"

"No, but that doesn't mean anything. He doesn't hang out with any girls, really. Maybe he's shy."

"Or maybe he's not worth it."

Mattie is silent.

"I just think you're too good for him," I say.

This perks Mattie up a little bit. "You're just saying that because you're my friend and you have to say things like that."

"No, it's the truth," I insist. "You were too good for Josh and you're too good for Declan."

"Well, we can't *all* be lucky enough to have Michael Greenblat fall in love with us," Mattie jokes.

I grab the sleeve of her jacket, glancing around the arcade wildly. "Shh, keep it down, someone might hear you!"

Mattie laughs. "You just don't want to admit it. Michael is in love with you."

"He is not."

Mattie rolls her eyes. "He is, too."

"What does love mean anyway?" I grumble.

"Fine. But he definitely likes you, and not like a friend, he *like*-likes you. Now you have to decide what to do about it. Do you like him?"

"Yes." This is the first time I admit out loud — to myself, Mattie, and whoever else is within earshot — that I like Michael Greenblat. And not just like him, but *like*-like him. It's not that bad. There's no fanfare, no flashing lights. I feel relieved and even a little bit liberated.

"Do you want to hang out with him?" Mattie asks.

"Alone?"

"Yes, alone."

"I guess so," I say, even though the thought of hanging out with him alone, in private, fills me with mild panic. What would we do, watch a movie? How closely should we sit together on the couch? Do we have to hold hands? Would there be kissing?

"Earth to Clarissa," Mattie says. "What's wrong with you? You look like you're going to be sick."

"I'm fine, I just don't know what I'm supposed to do next."

"At the very least you owe him a phone call."

"Why?"

"Clarissa, he told you he liked you, to which you responded 'that's good,' and then when he clearly wanted to kiss you, you ran into the house."

"I did not run."

"You basically did."

"Ugh! Why is this so hard?" I put my forehead in my hands, worst-case scenarios running through my head.

Mattie pats me on the shoulder. "Love is hard," she says dreamily. "Not that I'm speaking from experience. Until Declan realizes I'm perfect for him, I'll just have to keep living vicariously through you."

Now I'm the one doing the eye rolling. "If you're counting on Declan, you might have to wait a while," I point out.

Mattie pouts, crossing her arms. "I'm sick of waiting for love. Hurry up and get here already!"

"Good things come to those who wait," I say with a grin.

Mattie laughs. "Oh, please! You're the most impatient person I know!"

"Want to trade places?" I ask.

"I'd trade places with you in a second."

"Will you call Michael for me then?"

Mattie laughs. "You big baby. Just call him already!"

Call

Even after my conversation with Mattie, it takes me a while to work up the nerve to call Michael. I keep telling myself that he's the one who said "I like you" and that I have nothing to lose. It's already been a week since that night at Pizza Hut, and I've barely spoken to him. If I were him and I had said, "I like you," and the other person hadn't even called me, I'd be freaking out. But maybe only girls do that. That, plus the fact that my mom is in the middle of a perm and won't be able to interrupt me, makes me pick up the phone and dial his number. It rings six times before a man picks up — his dad?

"Hello?"

I clear my throat. "Um, yes, hello. Could I speak with Michael please?"

"Who is this?"

"It's Clarissa."

"Hang on a second, Clarissa. MICHAEL! THERE'S A GIRL ON THE PHONE! SOMEONE NAMED CLARISSA! IS SHE YOUR GIIIIIIIRLFRIEND?" Definitely not his dad. Maybe one of the three brothers?

I hear laughter and then something, possibly the phone, clatters. After an excruciatingly long time, Michael comes on the line. "Hello?"

"Hi, Michael. It's Clarissa."

"Oh, hi. How are you?"

"Good, how are you?"

"I'm good."

It occurs to me that this is as far as I had planned. What am I supposed to say now? I couldn't possibly just launch into any romantic stuff. I need a segue, and a good one. "So, you're good?"

"Yeah, pretty good. Baseball tryouts are soon, so I'm kind of nervous about that, but otherwise I'm good."

"Baseball?" I repeat. Cripes, is there any sport Michael doesn't play?

"Yeah. I'm thinking of trying out for a different team. It's still Little League, but it's a step up. There'll be more guys trying out; some of them will be a lot better than me."

"You don't know that. I'm sure you're just as good as those guys." I'm glad we're on the phone and that Michael can't see me blushing.

"Maybe, if I make the team, you could come to a game?" Michael says.

"Sure," I say, thinking, could this be date number two?

There is a pause in the conversation. Last year, Mr. Campbell taught us that every ten minutes there is a natural lull in conversation. Michael and I have only been talking for five minutes. I wonder if this is a bad sign. I take a deep breath and continue. "So, about Pizza Hut."

"Yes?"

"I'm sorry about the whole sharing a table with my mom thing."

"That's okay. It was kind of fun. But maybe we can get something to eat on our own sometime."

My heart is thudding so loudly I hold the phone away from me, just in case Michael can hear it. "Yeah, that's kind of why I was calling."

"Oh, yeah?"

"Yeah. To say that if you wanted to get dinner or lunch or any kind of food, really, that would be good." The minute it's out of my mouth I want to sink into the floor. Good? That would be *good?* I can't believe I said it again. Michael must think I am some idiot with a limited vocabulary.

I want to say more, but I'm interrupted by a beep. "Michael, there's a call on the other line. Do you mind if I take it? It might be someone calling to book an appointment at the salon."

"No problem. I'll just wait."

"Great, thanks."

I press the call-waiting button and take the second call. "Hello?"

"Clarissa, it's Benji."

I don't know why, but I immediately feel guilty, like I've been caught doing something wrong. "Hi Benji, what's up?"

"Are you busy?"

I'm not sure how to answer that, so I don't. "Why?" I ask instead.

"Charity was supposed to come over and help me with my song, but she has an audition. Apparently the casting director asked for her specifically," Benji says. I can hear the stars in his voice. "I really need a second opinion," he adds. "Can you come over?"

I don't much appreciate being second to Charity, but I bite my tongue. I think about Michael, waiting patiently on the other line for me. I don't want to leave him hanging, but it's not like we made any plans to hang out tonight. I told Mattie I would call him and that's what I did. Benji is so busy these days that I have to take any time I get to spend with him. Plus he needs my help. I'm sure Michael will understand.

"Can you give me one sec?" I ask Benji. I put him on hold and go back to the other line. "Hi, Michael?"

"Hey. Was it a client?"

"No, it was Benji. I have to go. He needs my help with something."

"Oh." Michael's voice sounds heavy.

I rush on, "It's for his play, *The Wizard of Oz.* He's the Cowardly Lion, remember?"

"Yeah, I remember. When is it? I really want to see it."

"In a few weeks."

"Maybe we can go together."

I think of all the people I know who will be there: my mom, Denise, Mattie. If Michael comes with me, there is no way around it, I'd have to introduce him and then the cat will be out of the bag. Everyone will know about "us," whatever "us" means. "Okay, sure."

"Well I guess you better go help Benji. It was really nice to talk to you, Clarissa."

"You, too. Bye, Michael."

"Bye."

"Hello, Benji?"

"Yes?"

"I'll be right over."

Lion

My phone call with Michael leaves me feeling light-headed and giddy, like my whole body is made of root beer or ginger ale or something fizzy. I have to walk it off before I am able to calm down and head over to Benji's. But when I arrive and see how anxious he is, the fizzy pop sensation goes flat.

He's downstairs in the den, seated at the edge of the big leather couch, his foot tapping like mad against the floor. He's wound so tightly that he practically springs off the couch when I enter. "Thanks for coming. You're my last hope," he says.

Last hope? My good mood deflates a little more. I know I'm not a professional actor like Charity, but I like to think that I have something useful to offer. "What's the matter?"

"It's my song," Benji confesses, looking truly miserable. "I know all the words, but the director says I'm not feeling it."

I don't know exactly what that means, but I don't like seeing Benji so distraught. It makes me hate Charity a little more, knowing that she was supposed to be here and now she's let him down. Just because she's a better actress than me doesn't mean she's a better friend.

"Let's try it from the top," I say, and Benji takes a deep breath and starts to sing.

I've heard him sing before, of course, but never thought

anything of it. Now that he's been handpicked to be in a musical, I pay much more attention. He has a nice voice, kind of quiet, and maybe a little high for a boy, but it's clear and natural.

When he finishes, Benji shoves his hands in his pockets, looks at me with his big eyes and asks, "Well? What did you think?"

"Honestly?"

"Of course, honestly," Benji says, but he looks nervous.

"You sound great, but it's not very Cowardly Lion, if you know what I mean."

"Okay . . ."

"I mean you're singing it like Benji, or like someone on the radio, not like a lion who is describing his dream."

Benji thinks about this for a second. "So, you think I need more character?" he asks.

"Yes!"

Benji nods thoughtfully, as if he was expecting this assessment of his performance. "Charity says you should approach your songs as an actor first and a singer second."

I am annoyed that even though she isn't here, even though *she* ditched *him*, Benji still quotes Charity like she is the ultimate authority. "Okay then, so how are you going to approach this song?"

Benji thinks about it for a second, then says, "Proudly? Like a king?"

"Here," I toss an old throw from the couch over his shoulders, "this can be your cape." Benji holds the throw blanket-cape closed around his neck and stands up a little taller. "That's it! Now try it again."

This time, Benji sings with his chin up and makes all sorts of grand gestures with his arms.

"Yes! That's it!" I cry, clapping wildly as he finishes.

"Clarissa, you're really good at this," Benji says.

"Oh, stop it," I say, but it makes me feel good.

"No, really. You could be a director!"

A director! I've never thought about that before. Come to think of it, that might be fun — calling all the shots, casting all the actors.

"Maybe you could assistant direct. Charity says that they're always looking for people to help at Gaslight Community Players."

There's that name again. Every time I hear it, it gets to me like a mosquito bite that won't quit itching. "Charity seems to know everything," I say curtly.

"What do you mean?" Benji asks.

"I mean she seems to be the be-all and end-all, where you're concerned."

"Well, she kind of is when it comes to acting. She's —"

"Professional, I know, you've told me!" I snap.

"Are you mad at me?" Benji asks, surprised.

"All you can talk about is Charity! Are you in love with her or something? Well she's not here now, is she? I am. Newsflash, Benji: She's in high school, she's a big star. She's never going to look at you as anything but a kid."

Benji is so genuinely shocked that his mouth hangs open and his makeshift cape slips to the floor. He looks nothing like a lion and everything like a person who has just had his feelings squashed by his best friend. I wish I could swallow those hateful words back up. I know he's not in love with her. I don't know what made me say those things. I'm so embarrassed I feel sick to my stomach. "She's my friend," Benji says eventually, lower lip quivering.

"I know, I'm sorry," I mutter.

But Benji isn't letting me off the hook yet. "You have other friends," he continues. "You hang out with Mattie all the time without me and I don't get mad at you."

"But she's your friend, too," I protest. "Besides, you'd be hanging out with us if you weren't at rehearsal all the time."

"I thought you were happy for me."

"I am."

"You don't act like it sometimes."

"I know, I just feel . . ." Jealous? Angry? Upset? I can't tell him any of that without looking like a big baby. ". . . I miss hanging out with you. It's not fair. Charity gets you all to herself."

"We're hanging out right now, aren't we?"

"Yeah, and look what happened. We're fighting!"

"You could hang out with us too, you know. I've invited you to come to the SAPS with me, but you just made fun of them."

"I know," I mutter. "I'm sorry. I just hate hearing about all the fun you're having. I wanted to be in this show too, remember?"

"I know," Benji says. "Don't get mad at me when I say this, but it's not my fault that you didn't get in. I wanted you to get in, too. If it wasn't for you, I wouldn't even be in the play. I never would have tried out if you hadn't made me."

Even though it feels good to hear him say that I am the reason he's in the play in the first place, it still doesn't make me feel any better about the whole situation. Benji continues, "I really, really like it, Clarissa, but I feel like I can't tell you about it because you'll get mad at me."

The whole ugly truth sits between us. It's more than just an elephant in the room, it's an elephant with a wonky eye and a gnarled tusk and oozing scabs all over its legs. We sit in silence, me braiding the tassels on the throw blanket and Benji doodling on the soles of his running shoes.

After a minute, Benji clears his throat and asks, "Is it okay if we keep practising? I think your suggestions are really making a difference."

I recognize an olive branch when I see one. "Sure! This time, I want you to wear this." I take off my headband and place it on Benji's head, like a crown. "I guess it's more like a tiara than a crown, but you get the idea. Now try it again."

Benji belts out his song again. This is the best he's sung it yet, complete with facial expressions and a lion-like prowl. He really is very good. I see why they cast him; he's a natural!

"What's going on down here?"

Benji stops singing mid-sentence. The Dentonator stands in the doorway, the TV guide in one hand, a can of beer in another.

Benji and I respond automatically. "Nothing."

"Doesn't sound like nothing," the Dentonator says.

"Well, not nothing, exactly —" Benji falters.

"We're rehearsing," I say.

The Dentonator scratches his right eyebrow with his pinky finger. "Rehearsing?" he repeats.

I roll my eyes. "You know, for the play?" Cripes, how thick can you be?

"It's for *The Wizard of Oz*," Benji says, "Remember? I'm the Cowardly Lion?"

"Yeah, yeah; I remember now. I didn't know there was singing in this play."

"It *is* a musical," I point out.

The Dentonator narrows his eyes and nods in Benji's direction. "What's that you've got on your head?"

141

Benji touches the headband. It slips over one eyebrow, like a fallen halo. "It's supposed to be my crown," he explains. "You know, because I'm the King of the Forest?"

The silence that follows is excruciating. Benji squirms as his father takes a long swig from his beer, never once taking his eyes off the headband that is now clenched in Benji's fist.

"Are there many boys in this play?" he finally asks.

"A few," Benji says.

"About how many?"

Benji shrugs. "I don't know, maybe four, five?"

The Dentonator's eyebrows disappear into his ball cap in disbelief. "*Maybe* four or five?"

"Five," Benji confirms.

"That's not very many."

"I guess not."

We all stand there, looking anywhere but at each other, until finally the Dentonator downs what's left of his beer. "Well, I guess I'd better let you get back at it."

"No, wait!" Benji says. The Dentonator pauses on the stairs. "Did you see the ticket order form I left for you? On the fridge?"

"I must have missed it," the Dentonator says. "Why?"

"We're supposed to bring our advance ticket orders in on Monday."

"Oh, right. When is this show of yours happening?"

"In three weeks. I wrote it on the calendar. There's a show every night from Wednesday to Saturday, with a matinee on Sunday."

"I've been working the night shift lately."

"I know, that's why I wanted to tell you now. So you can switch with someone." Benji smiles hopefully.

142

The Dentonator doesn't smile back. "It's not that easy, Ben. You can't switch just a single shift."

"I know. I thought if you had enough notice you could request to be put on days for that week."

For the third time in less than half an hour, an uneasy silence settles over the room.

"We'll see, Ben. I can't make any promises." The Dentonator turns and lumbers up the stairs. I wait until he has disappeared somewhere in the house before turning back to Benji and suggesting we start again.

"I don't feel like singing anymore," Benji says flatly.

"Want to watch a movie?" I ask.

Benji shakes his head. "No. I'm feeling kind of tired. Maybe you should go home."

I don't tell him that it's barely eight o'clock; instead I gather my things and head back to my house. Before I leave, I look over my shoulder and say, "Benji, you sound really great. You're going to make an awesome Lion."

Benji smiles but doesn't say anything. I know it's wrong to hate your best friend's dad, but sometimes I really hate the Dentonator. He has a way of making people feel small, especially Benji.

Bowl

When I get home, Doug is reading the paper at the kitchen table, frowning.

"What's the matter?" I ask. "Did your team lose?"

Doug shakes his head. "Nope. My teams are all rock-solid at the moment. It's this crossword that's driving me nuts. What's an eight-letter word for abdicate?"

I shrug. Puzzling over the crossword is something I picture old people or librarians doing, not a giant personal trainer with a mop of a dog named Suzy.

I guess my feelings were written all over my face, because then Doug says, "Why do you look so surprised? What, you think I'm all brawn, no brains?" Before I can protest, Doug continues, "I don't blame you, a lot of guys I know spend so much time on their pipes they don't bother with their noggins." Doug taps the side of his head. "But let me tell you something, the brain is just another muscle. It needs to be worked out just as much as your pecs or your gluteus maximus does. Do you know what the gluteus —"

"Yes, I know what the gluteus maximus is," I interrupt. It seems to be the only scientific muscle name that any of the boys in my class can remember.

"Of course you do, you're a smart girl. Anyway, doing the crossword every morning helps keep my brain in shape.

144

What good is keeping this in shape," Doug gestures at his body, "if your head isn't in top form?"

"Where's my mother?"

Doug nods his head in the direction of the bathroom. "Beautifying, not that she needs it."

Barf.

In the bathroom, my mom is humming as she applies what looks like a fourth coat of mascara.

"What's going on?" I demand.

"We're going out," Mom chirps.

"Have a good time," I mutter, starting to make my way to my bedroom.

Mom stops me. "No, I said *we're* going out. Doug is treating us."

"Us?" I repeat.

"Us," Mom confirms, slipping her arm around my shoulder. "Won't that be nice? We can all spend some time together, getting to know one another."

Nice is not exactly how I would describe that scenario. "Where are we going?" I ask warily.

"Bowling."

"Excuse me?"

Mom grins. "You know, bad shoes, ten pins, black light?"

"Doug is talking us to Shake, Rock 'n' Bowl?"

Just then, the devil himself calls from the kitchen, "The bowling train departs from the station in five minutes."

***

Five years ago, a late-night manager of a video store won the lottery and decided the only thing he really wanted in life was to own a bowling alley — but not just any bowling alley, a black-light bowling alley. And so Shake, Rock 'n' Bowl was built. It has ten lanes, real jukeboxes, custom bowling shirts you can order with your name stitched in red thread over the pocket and, of course, black lights. I've been there once before, for a birthday party, and found it seriously lacking in fun. As a date, it seems like a lame choice to me. Not that anyone else thinks so. Mom and Doug are positively giddy all the way there.

"I can't remember the last time I went bowling," Mom giggles.

Doug leans across to the passenger seat and squeezes her knee. "I'll go easy on you," he teases. Then he catches my eye in the rearview mirror. "Besides, it's Clarissa I'm going to have to watch out for. If those badminton skills transfer over to the lanes then we're both in big trouble."

I roll my eyes, not that the two lovebirds in the front seat take any notice.

It is surprisingly busy at Shake, Rock 'n' Bowl. I guess there really isn't anything else to do in town on a Friday night. How sad is that? Doug barters with the manager for a lane while Mom and I pick out shoes.

"You know, when we were kids we used to steal shoes from the bowling alley," Mom says, looking wistful. "Do you want brown with red laces or black with green laces?"

I take a pair of black with green laces and try to imagine why anyone would steal such ugly shoes.

Doug comes back, teeth glowing under the black lights. His jeans and shirt are dark, so he looks disturbingly like the Cheshire cat, his fluorescent smile floating somewhere in the region of where his face might be. "All right, ladies. Lane seven it is!"

Mom laughs. Doug pretends to look horrified. "What, do I have something in my teeth?" He hams it up, picking at imaginary food between his two front teeth. I don't get the appeal of black light. The novelty wears off after a few minutes. So what if your teeth and the lint on your t-shirt glow? It's also pretty hard to see what you're doing.

It turns out badminton is not the only useless sport I am good at; I am also a bowling pro-star. I win the first game, surprising everyone. Doug keeps offering his hand and saying, "up top, down low" or asking me to "give him some skin." How many lame ways can there be to say high-five?

Mom is having a rough go of it, slipping in her ugly shoes and tossing the ball into the gutter every other throw. She doesn't seem to mind, though; she laughs and cheers when Doug or I knock down pin after pin.

"How did my daughter get to be so good at bowling?" she teases.

"Clearly not from her mother," Doug says, winking. "Clarissa, you want to come over here and give your mother a few pointers?"

"Nah," I say. "I know a hopeless case when I see one."

Doug bursts out laughing and offers his hand yet again for a high-five. Without thinking, I reach out and slap his palm with mine.

Mom pretends to pout. "You two are picking on me."

"Okay, okay, time out." Doug waits for a smaller ball to spit out of the dispenser. He picks it up, walks over to my mom, and gives her a private lesson. Mom slips her fingers into the bowling ball and Doug stands behind her, puts his hand over hers, and guides her arm into proper bowling form. His other hand rests on her waist. He talks right into her ear and the two of them giggle like teenagers.

I can't hear them from the bench where I'm sitting, but that's fine with me. I slouch in my seat and take a few furtive glances in either direction. I am glad for the cover of black light. Everyone seems to be caught up in their own games and missing the spectacle going on in lane seven, thank goodness.

Finally, with Doug's help, Mom gets her first strike.

"Hey-o!" Doug high-fives my mother and lifts her into a bear hug, swinging her feet right off the ground. The foghorn sounds, cuing the strobe lights, which hit the disco ball in the middle of the bowling alley, showering the place with drops of light. Everyone looks over and smiles as my mom does what can only be described as her happy dance, like the ones bad actors do on lottery commercials.

"Mom, cut it out, people are looking."

"Let them look! I just got a strike!"

"Big deal, one strike."

"Your turn, missy."

Despite Doug's one-on-one attention, my mom is still a hopeless bowler and I come *thisclose* to winning the second game, losing by eight measly points to Doug.

"What do you say we play best two out of three?" Doug suggests. "Loser has to buy everyone ice cream."

Doug may be older than I am and a personal trainer, but he is also seriously distracted by my mother. Love may be great and everything, but it is a liability in bowling. I figure I have this one in the bag. "Deal."

Doug grins and we shake.

"I like how you've completely written me off," Mom says, rolling her eyes.

"If you win, I'll buy you ice cream for a month," Doug says.

Mom throws a mock punch and Doug staggers as if he's really hurt before grabbing her head in an arm-lock and threatening to muss up her hair. For one awful second, I think they might start wrestling.

"Guys! Can we just play? People are looking."

"All this winning is making me thirsty. Are you thirsty, Annie?"

Mom nods. "I could use some water."

Doug grabs his wallet from his back pocket and hands me a ten dollar bill. "Here, grab two waters and whatever you want for yourself. Thanks, Clarissa. You're a doll. And a good loser, too."

I snatch the bill from his hand and make my way to the restaurant in the corner. It's really more of a bar, with stools and a few sets of tables and chairs shoved against the wall. Two bottles of water doesn't even come to five dollars, so I decide to treat myself to something nice. According to the menu, I can get a hotdog, fries, nachos, or something from the vending machine. Some restaurant.

"Hi there, can I help you?" The waitress smiles at me. She has dimples and the same terrifying glowing teeth as everyone else at Shake, Rock 'n' Bowl. Even though her shirt has the name Shirley stitched across the pocket and her hair is pulled back and threaded through the hole in her cheesy Shake, Rock 'n' Bowl baseball cap, I'd recognize her anywhere. Charity Smith-Jones.

Dads

"Well? Have you decided what you'd like?"

"Charity!" I blurt out.

Confusion, or maybe it's panic, ripples across Charity's face.

"It's Clarissa, Benji's best friend?"

Charity blinks once and then smiles. "Oh, right, of course. I remember you. It's hard to recognize people under these stupid lights."

Is it just my imagination, or does Charity look nervous?

"So, how was your audition?" I try to keep my voice as sweet and genuine as possible without sounding too smug. Charity had backed out of coaching Benji because she said she had an audition, now here she was at Shake, Rock 'n' Bowl. Let's see her act her way out of this one.

To my surprise she leans forward and asks, "Can you keep a secret?" I am immediately suspicious, but more than anything I'm curious. What kind of juicy secret could a minor celebrity like Charity be hiding? "I didn't have an audition today," Charity confesses.

"Obviously."

"I had to work. Here."

"I don't get it," I say. "Aren't you an actress?"

"Of course I am!"

"Haven't you been in, like, a million commercials?"

Charity waves it off like it's no big deal. "It's only been a few. Everyone just thinks it's more because those Tim Hortons commercials play all the time."

Tell me about it. "So why do you have to work?"

"It's not really my choice."

"So you're being forced to work at a bowling alley against your will?"

Charity cringes. "Something like that." When I don't respond, she continues, "My stepdad owns this place." She must have seen the disbelief on my face, because she rolls her eyes and adds, "I know, totally embarrassing, right?"

"No," I protest, but I admit there isn't much conviction behind it.

"Well it is, and I hate it here, but it's a big deal to my mom and Mike does so much for me — driving me to Toronto for auditions and stuff — so I can't really say no."

"Right," is all I can say.

Just then, a customer steps up to the bar and orders fries. Charity slips into her smiling waitress act while I sit there trying to wrap my head around the news that Charity is the stepdaughter of the Shake, Rock 'n' Bowl guy. From what I can remember from the picture of him in *The Bugle*, he was short and kind of funny-looking, with big ears and scraggly hair. It's hard to imagine he has anything to do with glamorous Charity.

"Sorry about that," Charity apologizes, pushing a basket of fries toward me. "Fries? They're on the house. Anyway, not very many people know that I work here. That's why I told The Benj I had an audition today. I know that's kind of low, but I didn't know what else to say. I just couldn't get out of this shift."

"He was really worried about his song," I point out, rubbing it in just a little.

It works, because Charity looks genuinely guilty. "I know, I feel bad about it. But I told him I'd help him next week. He's doing fine, he just needs more confidence."

"That's what I told him," I say.

Charity smiles. "Maybe between the two of us we can convince him that he's going to be amazing."

Charity's smile is so infectious that I almost forget that she lied about having an audition. Almost. "Do you always tell people you have an audition when you have to work?" I ask pointedly.

"I've only had to make something up one other time," Charity admits. "Look, you and Benji are best friends, right?"

"Right."

"I know you don't owe me anything, but I'd really appreciate it if we kept this between us." I think about it, enjoying a moment of power, if only for a few seconds. "Please, Clarissa?"

"I guess," I agree.

Charity melts into a puddle of relief. "Oh thank you, thank you, thank you! I really owe you one, Clarissa. You must think I'm a terrible person. You probably never lie to your friends."

Not on purpose, I think. "You're not terrible," I say.

"That's sweet." Charity grimaces. "You know what *is* terrible? This place. When I go home I have to shower immediately to get the smell of the hotdogs out of my hair. It's like sweaty armpits crossed with old cheese." Now that the crisis has been averted, Charity is bright and sunny again. "So who are you here with?"

152

"My mom and Doug."

"Who's Doug?"

"Her date."

Charity smiles sympathetically. "And he brought you along to win you over, right?"

I nod. "Pretty much."

"That sucks. My mom dated all sorts of losers before she married Mike. One guy used to take me to his baseball games." Charity rolls her eyes. "I *hate* baseball."

"Doug has this stupid dog," I say. "I guess he thinks all kids like dogs."

Charity groans. "That's a classic, using pets to get to the kids. Do you like him?" I shrug. "Because if you don't, I can give you a few pointers on how to scare away potential stepdads. My brother and I had lots of practice."

"Really?"

"We scared this one guy away by pretending to be bed-wetters. Every morning we'd get up early and pour a glass of water in each of our beds and then burst into our mom's room crying about wetting the bed again."

"You actually cried?"

Charity looks offended. "What kind of actress can't cry on cue?" she says. Then, "Is that them in lane seven?" I look in the direction that Charity is pointing and sure enough, there they are, wrapped in each other's arms. "Are they slow-dancing?" she asks.

I shudder. "Looks like it."

Charity shakes her head. "Well then you'd better act fast. They look like they're headed for happily ever after."

"Do you like your stepdad?" I ask.

Charity pours herself a Coke and stirs the ice with her straw. "Not at first, but then again I didn't like any of the guys my mom dated at first. But Mike was nice. He did the dishes and brought home movies we all could watch. He buys me a chocolate chip muffin after every audition because he knows they're my favourite. . . . So, yeah, I do like him." Charity stops, frowning. "My real dad doesn't approve of me doing commercials. He thinks all child actors turn into drug addicts."

"Do you see him very often?"

"Every other weekend, a month in the summer. What about you?"

"Oh, my parents aren't divorced. I never knew my dad."

Charity stops stuffing her face with the french fries and looks at me like she's never really seen me before. It takes a second before she asks, "Is he dead?"

"More like dead-beat. He took off before I was born."

Relieved, Charity drains the rest of her Coke in one loud slurp. "Ouch," she says. "Do you like Doug?"

I think about it for a second. "I don't *hate* Doug."

Charity smiles. "That's a start." She tips her head in the direction of lane seven again. "You'd better get back to your game before they start making out."

I hop off the stool, grab the waters for Doug and Mom, and thank Charity for the fries.

"No worries," Charity says. "Thanks for keeping everything on the down low. You're a cool kid, Clarissa. I can see why Benji likes you so much."

Imagine that. Charity Smith-Jones thinks that I, Clarissa Louise Delaney, am worthy of coolness. This puts me in such a good mood that I don't even care when Doug beats me and I have to buy everyone ice cream on the way home.

Bill

Usually Denise takes my mom to her doctor's appointments. Mom doesn't like to go alone and it makes Denise feel useful, even if she does speed all the way there or offend the receptionist. So when Doug arrives in his zippy red car, I almost can't believe my own eyes.

"What is Doug doing here?"

"Doug's taking me to my appointment. Do you want to cut school and come?" Mom asks.

"No," I say. I always say no. Some people think that not knowing is the worst, but I like to not know bad things for as long as possible. That way, if the news is the worst of the worst, at least you had as much blissfully ignorant time as possible. And if the news is good, who cares? You've got good news! "Aren't *you* going with her?" I ask Denise, who is being eerily quiet.

"I gave her the day off," Mom says lightly.

Denise laughs, but it sounds a little strained. I steal a glance, and sure enough, the veins in her neck look about ready to pop out. "I have a ton of stuff to do," she says, waving her hand.

Outside, Doug leans on his car's sorry excuse for a horn. I've heard bicycle bells that sound angrier.

Mom drapes herself over Denise's shoulders and gives her three quick kisses on the cheek. "Love you, DeeDee."

Denise reaches up and pats my mother's cheek. "Go on. And you make sure that man takes you someplace nice for lunch." And then Mom's gone, leaving behind the scent of her coconut body butter and pink lipstick smudges on Denise's cheek.

"Well, kiddo, it's just you and me," Denise says with a sigh. "Feels familiar, doesn't it?"

I don't dignify that with a response. Instead, I watch Doug pull away with my mother in his shiny red car. "Is that car expensive?" I ask, nodding toward the now empty driveway.

"Mid-range, I'd say," Denise replies. "Although knowing that man, he probably talked himself into a sweet deal."

"Maybe he got it in the divorce," I suggest.

Denise snorts. "Clarissa, you are the devil's own child," she says, then adds, "You don't like him much, do you?"

Denise has stopped flipping through her magazine and is staring at me, waiting for my response. I am instantly wary. Denise has no loyalty to me; one careless word and she'll run squealing to my mother. On the other hand, she's been left here with me while Mom gallivants around town with a man. Men are kind of Denise's sore spot. Especially since the whole Dennis thing didn't work out.

"It's not Doug so much as the idea of Doug," I say, hoping that is cryptic enough to stump her.

But to my surprise, Denise nods. "I know what you mean," she muses. "But you know, when it comes to men, Doug Armstrong is as good as they come."

"Better than my dad?"

Denise freezes up. "Where did that come from?" she asks.

I shrug. "I don't know. I've never met him. I just wondered how he stacked up."

Denise looks uneasy. "Don't you think this is kind of a mother–daughter conversation?" she says.

"Please. You know Mom. She won't tell me anything. I want to know the truth."

Denise snorts. "The truth! You make it sound like there's some big, dark secret we're keeping from you."

"How do I know there isn't one?" I counter. "It's not like anyone ever talks about him."

"There isn't," Denise insists.

"So tell me about him. Just a little bit. Please?"

Denise looks uncomfortable. "I don't know, kiddo, it really isn't my place —"

"PRETTY please?"

"I do believe this is the first time you've ever begged me for anything," Denise teases.

I do my very best not to get indignant or mouthy by reminding myself of the larger things at stake. Namely, information. "Exactly," I say. "Which proves how serious I am."

Denise gets up and rummages in our top cupboard, otherwise known as the liquor cabinet. There's not much up there, but she must have found what she was looking for, because she adds a splash of something to her coffee before settling down at the table.

"Fine. But we're going to do this my way, got it?" Denise knocks back a swig of coffee before continuing. "You ask the questions and I will do my best to answer them. If you don't like the answer, well, tough. Don't take it out on me."

"I won't," I promise.

Denise leans forward, narrows her eyes, and points a

finger at me. As always, her nails are impeccably filed and polished. "Don't make me regret this. I don't want to hear about you looking him up on YouTube or wherever and running away like some TV movie of the week."

I trace an X over my heart with my finger. "I won't," I promise.

Denise swirls the contents of her coffee cup before taking another healthy gulp. "I'm ready. Shoot."

"What did he look like?"

Denise is incredulous. "What did he look like?" she repeats. "All these years and you want to know what he looked like? Can't you just Google him? You can find a picture of anyone these days."

When it becomes clear that I am not about to change my mind, Denise relents. "Fine. He was kind of wiry, but not in a scrawny way. Good skin, decent teeth. He had a big mop of hair that was always falling in his eyes." Denise snorts. "We thought it made him look poetic."

"Poetic," I repeat.

"Yup," Denise says, rolling her eyes. "Poetic. You know, the tortured romantic type. But I'd bet my life he never read a poem in his life."

"Why?"

"Don't get me wrong, he was a smart guy, but he wasn't all that interested in school, especially the gushy parts. And poetry was definitely something Bill Davies would have considered gushy."

I don't know if this is a good or a bad thing. "Was he a dog person?"

"Now what kind of question is that?"

"You said I could ask anything."

"I don't know. Next question."

"Did he want kids?"

"I can't honestly say, but I doubt it. No offense, kiddo, but a man that involved in himself doesn't have a lot of room in his life for other people."

"Why? What was he like?"

"He could be a real pain in the butt. Annie's parents weren't very impressed with him, that's for sure. They thought he was a real blowhard; all talk, no substance. Turns out they were right. But he was . . . charming, funny. Had a bit of a smart mouth, just like someone else I know . . ."

"Do I remind you of him?"

Denise cocks her head and really looks at me a moment before answering. "I guess there a few things," she says eventually.

"Like what?"

"Well that hair, for one. And you're smart like him." Denise laughs.

"What's so funny?" I demand.

"I was just thinking I'd pay good money to see the two of you square off," she chuckles. "Good Lord, what a showdown that would be! But just so you know, I'd put my money on you any day. You may have inherited your father's mouth, but you've got your mother's charms. And that, kiddo, is a deadly combination."

"How did he and Mom meet?"

"Like everyone meets in this dumpy little town; they met at a bush party. Your mom was from Sir John A., he went to Bennington. She was dating Steve Frechette at the time, but Bill took one look at your mother chewing out some senior for picking on a niner and that was it."

"What was it?"

"You know. *It*. Love. He had to have her. He asked her

out that night but she said no. He asked her out three more times before she agreed to meet him at the Dairy Bar for a milkshake." Denise smiles, remembering. "That night your mom came home, called me up, and said, 'DeeDee, that man could talk the black off a crow.'"

"Did you like him?"

"I liked him fine," Denise says. "But I like Doug more. Doug is nicer; he really listens to you when you talk."

"Okay, okay." I could sense we were getting off track. I don't need a list of Doug's attributes. "What happened? Why did they break up?"

Denise shrugs. "It wasn't one thing specifically. Near the end they used to fight like cats and dogs. Bill was jealous of all the attention your mom got, being a local celebrity and all. He also didn't like that she spent so much time taking care of her pageant queen duties. Your mom thought he needed to lighten up. And then one day he went to visit his uncle out west and he never came back. Your mom was well shot of him, so she never really pursued it. They drifted apart, like people do sometimes."

This was unsatisfying. How could something that was so great just fizzle out? "Why did she pick him?" I pressed. "If my mom had her pick of any boy, why would she pick him?"

Denise drains the rest of her coffee. "Oh, honey. You don't get to pick. That's one of the cruel ironies in life; love picks you. Or, I should say, love picks *some* of us. When's the last time I went speeding off with a man in a red car?"

I ignore that last comment. "Did she love him?"

"Of course she did. She loved him something fierce. But this thing with Doug is different. With Bill, she was just a kid. They both were. She was barely older than you —

160

Good Lord, do you know how old that makes me? I can't believe that; where does the time go?"

"You were saying?"

"Right. With Bill, it was like they were two crazy kids in love, stupid, really. But Doug — Doug is the first man your mother has loved as a woman. And that's a whole different story."

There's that word again. Love. You hear it every day, but when you really stop and think about what it means, it's too big to wrap your head around. You use the same word to describe your favourite song or a pair of shoes as you would to explain how you feel about the people who mean the whole world to you. How is that possible? Surely there are more words in the English language to describe the different kinds of love you feel. I've heard people say that the Inuit have fifty different words for snow, shouldn't that mean we have at least a hundred words to describe love? To Mattie it means the perfect kiss and poems and forever after. To Mom it means letting someone other than her best and oldest friend in the whole world drive her to an important doctor's appointment. But what does love mean to me? If Mom is in love with Doug, then what comes next? Will he move in? Will they get married? Love: little word, big consequences.

"Anything else?" Denise asks.

"No, I'm good," I say. "Thanks."

"Did you get what you were looking for?"

"I don't know," I say, and I mean it.

***

I spend the rest of the day in a fog. My head is full of new and surprising information. I'm having trouble digesting it all and paying attention in class. I've never given much thought to my father before. But now, with Doug hanging around, I can't help but wonder about him. Bill Davies, the man whose DNA I share.

"What's wrong?" Benji asks between classes.

"Nothing," I insist, but I can hear the distraction in my own voice.

"I saw your mom leave with Doug this morning," he continues. "Where were they going?"

"The hospital," I say.

Benji's eyes widen. "You mean she took Doug instead of Denise?" he asks. I nod. "I guess it's serious, then."

"I guess," I repeat.

"Weird," Benji says. "But good, right?"

"I guess," I say. I don't know if I like the fact that everyone is so on-board with the whole Doug and Annie thing. Even though I've never met him, I feel sorry for my dad. It's not like he has a chance; he's not here to defend himself against Team Doug. Plus, he's my dad — doesn't that automatically put me on Team Bill? Do I even have a choice?

"I wish my dad would get married again," Benji muses. "It would be nice to have a woman around the house."

"Who said anything about marriage? They just started dating."

"I know, but things move faster when you're a certain age."

I don't know how much more my brain can handle. "Can we please change the subject?" I ask.

"Sure," Benji agrees. "So what are you going to do about Michael?"

Cripes. I never thought I'd say this, but math class can't come soon enough.

Suzy

When I get home from school there is a message from Doug waiting for me. "Hidey-ho, Clarissa! Annie is doing me the honour of allowing me to take her to dinner and a movie in the big city, so we won't be back till later this evening."

I can hear my mother laughing in the background. "Hi, baby!" she says. "I'll bring you home a treat!"

A treat. Like I'm some kind of pet.

Doug continues, "I'm hoping you can do me a big favour and slip over to my house and show Suzy some love. Just let her run out back, give her some food — it's under the sink — and she'll be yours forever more. Thanks, Clarissa. I owe you!" And then he hangs up.

So now I'm stuck looking after Doug's stupid dog. It's not like he gave me much of a choice. I might as well get it over with now.

I give Benji a call to see if he wants to come with me, but all he can think about is his musical, which opens in a week. I've done my best to close my ears to all the play talk, which has been much worse lately because the show is so soon.

"Any other day and you know I'd come with you," he says. "I'm going to Charity's for pizza and an Italian line-run. Get it? Italian line-run, Italian food?"

"Yeah, I got it," I say, not entirely certain what an Italian line-run is. But if Benji's not going to explain it, I'm not going to ask.

"I have to be there, it's tradition."

"No worries!" I say, sounding much brighter than I feel.

Even Mattie is busy. "We're going out for a family dinner," she says, adding, "but I could ask if maybe you could come, too, and then we could go together afterwards."

"No, it's fine."

"Are you sure?"

"I'll be fine, Suzy is barely a dog," I reply.

"Call my mom's cell phone if you need me!" Mattie says, giving me the number.

"Thanks," I say half-heartedly.

***

The walk to Doug's house only takes fifteen minutes. This boggles my mind. All this time, the man of my mom's dreams has been living fifteen minutes away, and yet she only met him a few months ago. I wonder if they ever crossed paths before, like maybe he pulled in behind her at the gas station, or they were in line at Sobey's and shared a lame joke about the weather.

Assuming they *did* meet way back when, I wonder why they didn't feel a connection then. Maybe because Doug was still married and my mother was still committed to sacrificing her happiness for me, her ungrateful child. But if someone is the love of your life, shouldn't you realize it instantly?

I wonder where Michael fits into all this. Not that I would call him the love of my life or anything even remotely like that, but I've known him forever and never wanted him to kiss me before. As much as it pains me to say it, I guess Denise was right; love is strange.

Doug's house looks like any old house on the street: short, squat, brown bricks and slightly darker brown shutters. His lawn is nicely mown and there is an elaborate lattice-work patio wrapped around the front of his house. Probably he built it himself. Doug is always talking about the things he's made with "his own two hands." There are flyers stuffed into his mailbox, and since I am in the business of doing favours, I fish them out with the intention of setting them on his counter.

The spare key is exactly where Doug said it would be, inside the barbecue by the side door. When I questioned the logic of putting a key in a barbecue he confessed that this was his old barbecue and the real one was around back.

"So you keep the old barbecue just to hide your spare key?" I asked.

"Also to fool anyone who might be looking to steal a barbecue," Doug explained. "They see this one, take it, and have no idea that the real deal is safe and sound in my backyard."

"Is barbecue theft common in your neighbourhood?"

"That's not the point," Doug said. "The point is to always be prepared."

I take the key from the dummy barbecue and before I even open the door I can hear Suzy chirping. You can't really describe the noises she makes as barking — it's too high-pitched.

"Calm down," I mutter. "It's just me."

I can't open the door too widely, or Suzy will explode into the yard. It requires a significant amount of agility to slide into the house through a small crack between the door and the wall. I enter with one foot in front of me, so I can push

Suzy aside while I slip in. The second I'm inside she starts jumping in funny little arcs; she reminds me of these little cartoon goats I saw on TV once, leaping from cliff to cliff. It's almost cute.

Just as Doug said, Suzy's food is in the cupboard directly under the sink. I probably could have figured it out myself. After covering my ankles in wet dog kisses, she trots straight for the cupboard where her food is kept and flops down in front of it, looking back at me through her doggy bangs with sad, hungry doggy eyes.

"Okay, okay."

She starts chirping again and weaves between my feet as I head over to her dish. Stupid dog. Doesn't she know I would get there faster if I wasn't worried about tripping over her and falling to my death? I have to move Suzy aside with my foot in order to open the cupboard. Once the food is in her dish she ignores me completely, chomping away on her premium brand puppy chow.

With Suzy occupied, I find myself with an opportunity to look around Doug's house. I'm sure if Doug was here he would give me the grand tour, and I'm certain he would want me to feel at home, so I slip off my shoes and take a look around.

Nosy

I've never been in a bachelor's house before, unless you count Benji's house, which isn't the same because his dad is a widower with a son, not a bachelor. I feel a little bit like Goldilocks, trying all the rooms on for size. It's cleaner than I expected, but it's definitely missing what my mom would call a woman's touch. If you ask me, it's missing any kind of touch at all. The walls are bare, except for a few concert posters. The kitchen is stocked with powdered protein shakes, energy bars, boxes and boxes of whole wheat pasta, a spotty bunch of bananas, and six different kinds of cereal.

In the living room, an enormous flat screen TV takes up most of one wall, across from which is a boring couch and an equally boring chair in a shade Benji would call écru but most people would call beige. If you look closely, you can see flecks of brown and grey in the weave. A low bookshelf sits under the bay window. It's full of self-help books with a fitness or diet theme, which I assume he uses for his work as a personal trainer. But there are some surprising titles, too, like the Scrabble dictionary and a couple of thick novels written by authors whose names look Russian or some other language that is equally complicated.

Downstairs, the basement is divided into three rooms. The ceiling is low. It's hard to picture a man as tall as Doug walking around comfortably down here. For the most part, it's full of basement-y stuff. There is a room full of old exercise equipment and even more books on diet and fitness regimes; a laundry room with three different types of detergent; and a plastic waste basket full of oddly purple-tinted lint. Coolest of all, there's a den with dark wood panelling and one of those old-time bars at one end. It even has red-topped swivel stools and a wooden cup full of plastic swizzle sticks — the kind you would spear a cherry or an olive with and drop into a fancy drink — sitting on the swirly silver and black countertop. It looks perfect for a party, like something out of a movie.

Mom is always complaining how there is no proper room in our house for entertaining. I never understood why she felt the need to entertain when she sees people all day long in the Hair Emporium, but this is just the kind of room she would love. She probably wouldn't love how dark it is, but I imagine she would find a way to lighten it up. She has the kind of woman's touch Doug's house is missing. I imagine her down here, entertaining, a glass of wine in her hand, the life of the party. All of a sudden the room feels too dark, the ceilings seem too low, and I can't get out of there fast enough.

There is only one room I haven't checked out. It's the only one in the whole house with a closed door. I'm assuming it's Doug's bedroom. There was only one other room with a bed in it, and it looked like no one had slept in it for years. I put myself in Doug's shoes; how would I feel if Doug went into my bedroom? As far as I know, Doug has never been near my room. I would definitely flip if he went in without my permission. Then again, he's dating my mother, so I figure that makes us even.

Doug's bed is enormous, covered in a navy blue duvet that is hunched up in a way that, if I didn't know any better, I might think there was someone still sleeping under it. At the foot of the bed is a fat, pink cushion in the shape of a donut. It's fuzzy in places and chewed up in others, and by the amount of wiry hairs that cling to it, I assume it's Suzy's bed. He lets her sleep on his bed? Barf.

A big, solid-looking dresser in honey-coloured wood is littered with all sorts of man-type things I'm not used to see-ing: an extra-large stick of triple-strength deodorant; bottles of aftershave and spicy-smelling cologne that make my eyes water; a plastic comb like the kind old-fashioned barbers use; a handful of change; and a big, waterproof watch. There is also a framed photo of Suzy sitting in the grass, cocking her head in that way that dogs do in pet food com-mercials when they are trying to be cute. Other than a few stray hairs clinging to the comb and some pocket lint mixed in with the change, I have to admit it's pretty clean.

In the closet, shirts and sports jerseys hang next to pants, neatly folded over hangers. Below them, on the floor, rows of shoes are lined up, toes pointing forward. On the top shelf in the closet are shoeboxes stacked one on top of the other. Aha! Jackpot. If I want to discover something private about Doug, a shoebox in a closet is the best place to start. It's not going to be easy getting them down from there, though. There aren't any chairs or anything else to stand on in Doug's room. I'll have to drag one in from the kitchen.

It's one thing to walk around someone's house, but going to the effort of dragging in a chair so I can reach his stash of shoeboxes and riffle through their contents is another story. I have gone from Goldilocks to full-fledged spy. Oh, well. It's not like I've never dabbled in a life of crime before, with my record of forgery, which Mr. Campbell so kindly erased, and blackmail, which led to the downfall of Terry DiCarlo, who had it coming anyway.

I drag a chair from the kitchen and position it in front of the closet. Perfect, I can just reach the top box. I take them all down, making a mental note of the order in which they were stacked. If I'm going to be a spy, I might as well be a good one. Doug will never know I've been in here; unless, of course, I discover incriminating information, in which case I'll probably have to reveal my source in order to prove my allegations. I'm feeling jittery, from my insides to my hands, which shake a little as I open the first box and find . . . receipts. Piles and piles of receipts, neatly bundled together with paperclips. At first I think maybe I'll find something interesting, like a house in Bali or some embarrassing operation, but they all appear to be business-related: photocopying expenses, lunches, and some course called, "Is Your Business Fit?"

The next shoebox is a little more interesting — newspaper clippings about Doug's gym and cards from former clients. I only read a few of them before I start to get bored. Doug must be really good; why else would you send your personal trainer a Christmas card? I'm not even halfway through them when I push the box aside and reach for the next one. I don't know what kind of dirt I expected to find in there. It's not like people hang on to hate mail. So far, I haven't found anything interesting, let alone scandalous. It's disappointing. Doug is just a regular, boring guy who likes fitness and cereal and lets his dog sleep on his bed. There are no skeletons in his closet, only boxes and boxes of receipts and business plans. I put the boxes back and survey the bedroom.

The only other place I could check is under the bed. I would have kept looking, but the sound of the screen door banging shut catches me off guard.

I freeze, straining to hear footsteps or a voice, but I can't hear anything over the rush of blood in my ears. I am flooded with red hot shame as I imagine Doug walking into his room and discovering me on the floor, riffling through his personal stuff. Barely daring to breathe, I stand up and inch my way silently toward the door. There are no signs of life in the hallway. Surely if someone had come in they would have said something by now?

And that's when it hits me. Here I am, worried about someone coming in, when what I should be worried about is someone — or something — getting out. Specifically, Suzy.

Lost

Sure enough, Suzy is nowhere to be found.

"Suzy? Suzy! C'mere, girl!" I burst through the side door, but Suzy is long gone. "Suzy? Are you in the backyard?"

I let myself into the backyard through the gate and creep around the perimeter, peering into the bushes and behind the shed, making the kind of soft, encouraging noises I've heard other people use when calling animals. It's getting darker out and every dog-sized shadow makes my heart jolt.

"Suzy?" But she's nowhere to be found. No paw prints, no barking, no nothing. Full-fledged panic sets in, and I tear out the backyard and into the street. "Suzy? SUZY!"

"Is that Doug's dog you're hollering after?"

I spin around like a wild thing to see an old man leaning on the fence, peering intently at me. "Yes," I say breathlessly. "I came over to feed her and she got out."

The old man chuckles. "Yep. She's a runner, that one."

I resist the urge to scream or tear at my hair and say as calmly as the situation allows, "Did you happen to see where she ran to?"

"Nope, but if I were you I'd head that way. There's a house with some of those ugly garden gnomes in the flowerbeds, number six-oh-five or six-oh-seven. That's Susan Larson's place." The old man points down the road, near the cul-de-sac. "Mrs. Larson usually keeps her dog Mr. Ruffles tied up out back and the last I saw him, he was giving Suzy a real good sniff in the behind, if you catch my drift." He chuckles again and shakes his head. "Good luck, girly."

So Suzy is a runner *and* boy crazy. Wonderful.

"Thanks," I say, and I jog down the road toward Mrs. Larson's house. "Suzy! Here, Suzy!"

The lights are on inside Mrs. Larson's house and an orange and white cat is sitting in the bay window, staring at me. It blinks slowly, as if in disgust. I don't blame it. I am disgusted at myself, running after that stupid hairball of a dog. I can't believe I didn't shut the side door properly.

I patrol the bushes beside Mrs. Larson's driveway, but there is no sign of Suzy. I feel weird about going into someone's backyard — after all, one can only commit so many crimes a day — so I ring her doorbell and hope desperately that Suzy is out back flirting with the unfortunately named Mr. Ruffles. I mean, Ruffles is bad enough, but *Mister* Ruffles? I bet he's a poodle with one of those ridiculous haircuts, and Mrs. Larson is probably eighty years old, bakes award-winning apple crisp, and has pink sweatshirts with photographs of her dog printed on them.

So you can totally understand why it takes me a moment to respond when Michael Greenblat opens the door and says, "Clarissa? What are you doing here?"

I stare.

"Clarissa?" Michael repeats.

When I'm able to speak, the only thing that pops into my head is, "You're not Mrs. Larson."

Michael looks at me funny. "No, want me to get her for you?"

"What are you doing here?"

Michael smiles. "I asked you first."

"Right. I'm looking for a dog."

"You didn't tell me you had a dog!"

"I don't, it's not mine. It's Doug's."

"Doug, your mom's boyfriend?"

Oh how I wish I could correct him, but this time there is no doubt about it; it's true. "Yeah. Her name is Suzy. I heard she has a crush or something on Mr. Ruffles, so I thought I'd check here."

Michael laughs. "Yeah, Ruffles is a bit of a ladies' man. All the bitches in the dog park totally love him."

I am horrified. "Excuse me?"

Michael sees the look of disgust on my face and rushes on. "That's what you call female dogs, bitches. It's the proper term for them. I didn't mean, you know, like, *bitches* . . ." he trails off lamely, scratching the back of his head as if that will erase the memory of what just happened.

I decide to give him the benefit of the doubt and change the subject. "Well, anyway. She got out and apparently she's a runner and now I have to find her before Doug gets back. Do you think we could check and see if maybe she's out back with Mr. Ruffles?"

"Sorry, Clarissa, but Mr. Ruffles is inside," Michael apologizes, adding, "but we can still check if you want."

I shrug, totally and completely defeated. "Sure. Might as well."

Michael holds the door open for me. "Come on, we can cut through the house."

"You still haven't told me why you're here," I remind him.

"Oh. Mrs. Larson is a friend of my grandmother's. I come over once a week to help her with stuff around the house, you know, like the garbage or vacuuming. Sometimes I take Mr. Ruffles for a walk."

"That's nice."

Michael shrugs. "It's no big deal."

"It's kind of a big deal," I insist. "I don't know any other people in our class who would do that, especially the boys."

"I get paid, a little. It's a job, not like I'm this do-gooder boy scout or anything." Michael looks annoyed, like I insulted his manhood instead of giving him a compliment. I just don't get boys.

"Well, here we are." Michael takes me through a little kitchen completely decked out in duck paraphernalia — duck dish towel, duck tea cozy, plaster ducks on the walls — and out the back door onto a porch. After being in a well-lit house, it takes a moment for my eyes to adjust to the dusky blue of the evening. I see a birdbath, an empty doghouse, and a recycling bin, but no Suzy. Everything in my chest tightens. It's been at least ten minutes. How far can a dog go in ten minutes?

"Sorry, Clarissa," Michael says.

"What should I do?" I ask him. "Is there someone I should call? I don't know anything about dogs." My voice is alarmingly shaky. Oh, God, please don't let me cry now, not in front of Michael.

"You could call the Humane Society, but it's too early for that. I'm sure she's around here somewhere. Did you check the park?"

I shake my head, no. I don't trust myself to speak.

"I'll come with you. I just need to get my coat."

Without a word, I follow Michael back through the duck kitchen, into the hallway, and out onto the front porch. I sit on the steps taking steadying breaths and wait for him to say goodbye to Mrs. Larson. I will myself not to cry. The concrete of the porch is cold beneath me and with the sun down, there is a nip in the air.

"Okay, let's go." Michael is back, carrying a large sweater. "Here, Mrs. Larson got this for you. It's kind of cold out," he says, offering me the sweater.

"Thanks, I am a little chilly," I admit. The sweater is pale pink, shapeless, and has a faded picture of a pond peeling off the front, complete with mallard ducks and cattails. It is exactly the kind of old lady sweater one would expect a woman who has a dog named Mr. Ruffles to own. Oh, well. Ugly sweater is better than no sweater. I pull it over my head. It falls about mid-thigh, the sleeves ending at the tips of my fingers. I wrap my arms around myself and head out into the darkness after Michael.

"We should knock on people's doors on the way to the park, just in case they saw her and brought her in," Michael suggests.

"Whatever you say," I agree.

And so we stop at every house, asking if anyone caught sight of a little white mutt tearing across the neighbourhood in the last half hour. At each place it's the same, "No, sorry. Good luck finding her!"

Some people recognize Michael as the nice kid who helps Mrs. Larson around the house. They are extra-sympathetic. "Sorry, Michael. We'll for sure keep an eye out for her!"

"It's no use," I moan.

Michael is determined. "Don't give up yet," he says. "There's still the park. It's a major hangout for dogs."

"If you say so," I sigh.

Michael tries to cheer me up by telling me all about homing instincts, and how even runners like Suzy know how to find their way home. He is full of stories of lost dogs who find their way home eventually. "Like this one dog was on vacation with his family in Florida and got lost. He showed up at their front door in Oregon two years later. Can you believe that?"

I frown. "Is that a true story?"

"You don't believe me?" Michael asks.

"It sounds a little like *The Incredible Journey*."

Michael smiles. "I bet *The Incredible Journey* was based on a true story, too. There are, like, entire books on amazing dog stories."

I don't have much to say to that. Clearly Michael has not met Suzy. Would an amazing animal run away from her warm home full of food and into the dark, cold night? Although I have to admit, ever since Michael agreed to help me look for Suzy, I've been feeling much, much warmer.

Park

"Well, here we are."

The park is really the playground at St. Patrick's Catholic school, or St. Paddy's as it's known around here. It is definitely the nicest park in the city. Not only does it have the usual climber and swing set, but it also has a set of teeter-totters, a tube slide, a tire swing, and the only merry-go-round in town. Plus the whole thing is bordered by tall pine trees that block out the sight of any houses. It feels like you're inside a fortress, a secret fortress of fun. It definitely beats the playground at Ferndale.

I guess dog lovers like the fact that the playground is surrounded by trees, too. It means they can let their dogs off their leashes and not worry too much about bothering the people who live behind St. Paddy's, although there aren't too many dogs around at this time of night.

"Let's check the border first," Michael suggests. "I'll go to the far side and you start here."

So we split up, searching in and among the trees. Michael whistles and I call Suzy's name, slapping my thighs and wishing I had brought treats or something to entice her with. I hear barking a few times, but it's always some dog behind the school, in a yard nearby. My heart leaps every time I hear barking, only to let be let down again and again.

When we meet in the middle, Michael smiles hopefully at me. "Any sign of her?"

"No," I grumble.

Michael frowns. "We have to think like Suzy. Where would you go if you were her?"

"Suzy doesn't think all that much," I say.

I make my way toward the merry-go-round, dragging my feet through the dust, the sleeves of Mrs. Larson's ugly sweater hanging almost to my knees. It smells like old lady and makes my nose itch, but at least I'm warm.

I sit with a thump, the merry-go-round making a satisfying clang that echoes in the now empty park. Michael joins me and does his best to cheer me up. "There has to be something we're missing. Dogs are motivated by rewards, like food or attention."

"I fed her ten minutes before she escaped," I point out.

"Maybe there was another dog or a rabbit or something that got her attention outside," Michael suggests.

"Okay, so then what?"

"I don't know," Michael admits. "I'm just thinking out loud."

I heave another big sigh and lay on my back in my quarter of the merry-go-round. The stars are starting to come out of hiding. I try to pick out one of the constellations, but I'm having trouble concentrating. I know I should be thinking about Suzy, and I am, but I'm also thinking about Michael, who has laid back on the other side of the merry-go-round and now our heads are almost touching.

"Do you know anything about constellations?" Michael asks.

"Not really, do you?"

"Sure!" Michael props himself up by his elbow and starts

pointing things out to me. "See there? That's the Big Dipper. Once you find that you can find anything." Michael rattles off the history of the different constellations, and I zone out, enjoying the sound of his voice. "What's your astrological sign?" he asks.

"Why? Do you believe all that stuff about astrology?"

"No," Michael sounds indignant. "I was just going to point out your constellation for you."

"Aries."

"It's hard to see Aries in the spring."

"How come?"

"That's when it's closest to the sun."

"What sign are you?" I ask. I feel dumb the second the words come out of my mouth. That sounds like a pickup line Denise would use.

"Virgo. It's easier to see it when it's really late, like midnight."

"I should probably be home by then," I say.

"Yeah, me too," Michael says. He sounds disappointed.

For a moment I wonder if he's going to get up and say it's time to leave. I don't want to leave yet, and not just because sudden death might be waiting for me at home. I need to stall him. "How did you learn to pick out the constellations?"

"I have a telescope and some books at home."

"Cool."

Michael twists around to look me right in the eye, like he doesn't believe me. "Really?"

"Really," I say, a little offended. "I like astronomy. I even have those glow-in-the-dark stars on my ceiling and everything." I don't mention that they no longer work.

Michael smiles and it feels like I swallowed a whole box of Pop Rocks that are exploding all over my body. I think

I could be happy for the rest of my life if only he would continue to smile at me like that. Oh how I wish I wasn't wearing an old lady sweater with ducks on it that reeks of baby powder.

"Do you ever read the horoscopes in the paper?" I ask.

"Maybe once in a while, out of curiosity."

"Me, too," I admit. "Sometimes they're pretty accurate."

"That's kind of weird."

"It is. What time is it?" I ask.

Michael consults his watch. "Almost nine. I should probably head home."

"Me, too" I sigh.

"Do you want me to come with you?" Michael asks. I do, but there is no reason why he should have to witness the smackdown that I'm sure is about to come.

"No, it's okay," I lie.

"I'll walk with you," Michael offers.

Home

We check at Doug's house one more time before heading back to my place, just in case Suzy decided to come home. No such luck. At least this time I remember to lock up behind me. I already lost Doug's dog. The last thing I need is for his house to be robbed, too.

"That old man said she was a runner, right?" Michael says.

"Yeah."

"So she must get out all the time. Doug is probably used to it."

"Maybe," I say, but I am not convinced.

"And she has ID tags, so even if she gets picked up by the pound, they'd still have a way to contact Doug. Even if the worst happens and she gets hit by a car, it wouldn't be your fault. You can't help it if it's in the dog's nature to run away. Besides, it's not like you were driving the car."

In my worst nightmares, I had never imagined Suzy being hit by a car. I'm starting to feel woozy. I know Michael is trying to make me feel better, but it's not working. I've been in Doug's bedroom, the only photo he has displayed is of Suzy. If she does end up dead on my watch, he's not likely to forgive me. And neither is my mother.

In my desperation I consider running away, too. Then everyone would be so worried about me that no one would think about the dog. In a perfect world I would spend the night searching and arrive on the doorstep, rumpled but alive, with Suzy in my arms. I would even be willing to make something up about how the dog found me and led me home. Then Suzy would be the hero, I would be alive, and everyone would be happy. Of course there are more than a few flaws in this plan. Anyone who has spent any time with Suzy would not believe her to be capable of rescue. She can barely fetch.

"Looks like they're home," Michael says. The lights are on in the kitchen and Doug's little red sports car is parked in the driveway. Time to face the music.

"Are you sure you don't want me to come with you?" he asks again.

"It might be nice to have a witness in case one of them tries to kill me," I say.

Michael looks uncomfortable.

"I'm kidding," I confess. "But, if you're sure you don't need to head home —"

Michael shakes his head. "I don't have to be home yet. Come on. We might as well get this over with."

It takes an unbelievably short amount of time to walk from the sidewalk to the door. I cast a glance at Benji's house, but it's completely dark. No rescue there.

"Here goes nothing," I say, partially to myself, partially to Michael.

I go to turn my key in the lock but the door swings open and suddenly Doug is there, blotting out the light with his enormous bulk.

"Clarissa! Where've you been?" Before I can answer, he continues, "Well get in here, we've been waiting for you." Doug spots Michael and ushers him in, too. "The more the merrier. It's a party in here!" And then he throws his head back and crows like a rooster.

At my side, Michael whispers, "Is he always like that?"

I shake my head. "No."

In the living room I can hear Mom and Denise laughing over an old record I haven't heard in ages. I forget all about being terrified or guilty. "What's going on?" I demand.

Doug grins at me, eyes shining. He looks insanely happy. Unhinged, even. "What's a nine-letter word for the best day of your life?" he asks.

"Christmas?" Michael guesses.

"No," I say. "Remission."

***

The living room is full of light and music. There's only five of us but it feels like more. Mom keeps pulling out albums she hasn't heard in ages and putting them on the record player. The record only plays for a few songs before she finds another album. She stops the record mid-song so she can replace it with the next one. Each song is the kind of song you've heard on the radio your entire life — you don't know what it's called, but somehow you know all the lyrics. Even Michael nods his head and sings along.

Doug produces half a cheesecake in a flimsy white box, left over from his dinner with Mom, and we attack it with forks, forgoing plates altogether. I manage to find a few cans of root beer for Michael and me while the adults open the bottle of wine my mom bought especially for this occasion.

Remission. I've been saying it to myself for months and now I can finally say the word out loud. "Remission."

The dreamy look slips from Mom's face. "What did you say?"

"Remission," I repeat, this time a little louder. "Remission, remission!"

Mom sits next to me on the couch, placing a hand firmly on my knee. "Clarissa, the doctor didn't say 'remission.'"

The cheesecake forms a solid lump in my stomach. "But . . . I thought — Doug said . . ."

Mom frowns at Doug, who looks sheepish. I've never seen her send anything but a smile in his direction before. That's when I know she's serious. "The doctor said that at this point, I'm cancer-free," she explains. "Doug should have been clearer."

I don't understand. How is being cancer-free different from remission? "Isn't that the same thing?" I ask.

"Not exactly."

"So you could get sick again?"

"I could. But I'm not planning to." Mom winks at me.

Just when I thought the coast was clear, another cloud moves over the horizon. "Then what's the point?" I say.

Mom thinks before responding. "The point is, anyone can get sick at any time. Right now I'm healthy. That's good enough for me."

I search Mom's face for any sign that she's pretending to be strong for my sake, but all I see is relief — honest-to-goodness relief. She isn't hiding anything from me and if cancer-free is good enough for her, then it should be good enough for me. Nothing is ever sure in life, I know that now. You never know when people will get sick or when they will take offense at something you did. You can do everything right and still things will go wrong. Life is full of surprises. But not all surprises are bad.

"Okay," I say.

Mom leans in for a bone-crushing hug. Across the room,

Denise laughs and cries and sloshes her drink all over the couch and herself. But Mom is too giddy to notice. She looks lit from within, as if a hundred tiny candles are flickering under her skin. She gets up and starts calling people to let them know the good news. She holds the phone out and says, "Say hi, everyone!" and dutifully, we respond, "Hi everyone!" and then burst into fresh laughter. I smile so hard it feels like my cheeks are going to split, but I can't stop.

If anyone was to look in on us right now they would think we were a group of crazy people, and that's just how I feel, crazy-happy. I hold onto this feeling as long as I can, but things wind down and I can't keep putting off my talk with Doug. I feel like I'm holding onto a full balloon and the air is rushing out, and I'm about to be flung around the room.

"What's wrong?" Michael asks.

"I still have to tell him," I confess, nodding at Doug who is doing an impression of the snooty waiter he and Mom had at the restaurant. Denise laughs so hard she snorts. I hope wine doesn't come out of her nose.

Michael nods gravely. "That sucks," he sympathizes. "But at least he's in a good mood."

"I guess," I sigh.

"Good luck," Michael says gravely.

I wait for the impression to be over and then I follow Doug into the kitchen, where he fills the empty ice trays with fresh water. "Doug, I have to tell you something."

"You look serious."

I swallow before answering. "It is serious."

"Okay, shoot." Doug turns off the tap, sets the trays down, and tries to look all solemn and sober, but I can tell by the faraway look in his eyes and the smile that keeps trying to break out across his face that he's still thinking about my mom and how she's out of the dark and he's probably planning the rest of their lives in his head. Or maybe that's something only girls do.

I lead him over to the kitchen table and we sit down. "It's about Suzy," I begin.

"Suzy Q! How is the little rascal? Did she give you any trouble?"

My throat is dry, but my root beer is nowhere to be found. "Well, the thing is, I fed her and everything, but my back was turned for a minute and she sort of . . . escaped. I didn't know she was a runner, so I didn't think about checking the screen door."

To my surprise, Doug slaps his thigh and laughs. "That rascal! I should have warned you, she'll do anything to get out of the house. Did you find her at the Larsons'?"

"Well I checked, but she wasn't there." I falter and look over at Michael for strength. He is sitting on the edge of the couch clutching his root beer and smiling politely as Denise yammers on about something. He catches my eye and smiles. I take a deep breath. "The thing is, I couldn't find her. Michael and I looked everywhere. She's gone." I hold my breath and wait for the axe to fall.

Doug looks thoughtful. "When did this happen?" he asks.

"Around seven-thirty? Maybe eight?"

Doug checks his watch. "I bet you she's crying at my side door this very minute."

"Really?"

"I'm sure of it. She never goes far and she always comes back." Doug stands. "I should probably go let her in."

"So, you're not mad?"

"Heck, no! If I'm mad at anyone, it's myself. I should have told you she would try to sneak out on you. And now you've been running around looking for her, probably worrying yourself sick."

I shrug, even though I want to scream, "Yes, yes, that's exactly what I've been doing!" I ask, "What if she isn't there?"

"She will be," Doug says, winking. "I'll bet you the last piece of that raspberry cheesecake."

"But what if she isn't?" I insist.

"If she isn't, I will call the pound tomorrow and make some flyers with her silly little mug on it and someone will find her and return her. There aren't a lot of people who would put up with a Tasmanian devil like her."

I'm not convinced that Doug is thinking this through completely. "And what if nobody brings her in?"

Doug puts his hand on my shoulder and looks me right in the eye. When he speaks, his voice is low and serious. "Clarissa, I had the most amazing experience in that doctor's office with your mother today. Sometimes we forget what a gift life is. Today, I was reminded of that. There are some things that are worth worrying about, and some things that aren't. I'm sure Suzy is at my door right now, flopping that little tail of hers in the dirt. I want you to come with me so I can prove it to you, and you won't worry your pretty little head about it anymore."

"Okay," I agree.

Doug nods his head at Michael, who looks uncomfortable as Denise examines his nail beds. "Go rescue our pal Mikey over there. He can come with us and then I'll drive him home."

Glee

I'm too anxious to talk on the way back to Doug's house. It feels like everything from the neck down, not just my stomach, is tied up in knots. Thankfully Doug is still high on life and cruises with his arm hanging out the open window, singing along to the radio, even though he doesn't know the words. Michael, sitting in the passenger seat, laughs, and then Doug laughs along with him. Men. It's like they're completely oblivious to the agony I'm going through back here.

As we pull in and the headlights sweep over the driveway, I catch a glimpse of something white at the side door. Once it starts to bark and run in circles, there is no doubt that it's Suzy. I am so relieved I practically melt into the seat.

Doug grins at me. "Looks like someone owes me a piece of cheesecake."

I manage to let myself out of the car and follow him and Michael to the house.

"C'mere, you crazy girl!" Doug calls. Suzy is frantic with love and launches herself at Doug who lifts her up and lets her attack his face in sloppy dog kisses. Ugh. "You're a bad girl, Suzy Q, running away on Clarissa like that! Bad, bad girl!" But he is laughing as he says it and Suzy is concentrating too hard on barking and licking Doug's face at the same time that I doubt she realizes she's being scolded.

"I'm going to let this rascal in and I'll be right out to drive you home, Michael." Doug disappears into the house, Suzy weaving in and out of his legs, still barking like a possessed creature. Michael and I are alone in the driveway. I am dizzy with relief.

"Pretty crazy night," he says.

"You can say that again."

"Pretty cool, too."

"Really cool." A shiver travels down my spine all the way to the tips of my toes. When I go to wrap my arms around myself, I realize that I am still wearing Mrs. Larson's hideous sweater.

"I should give this back to you so you can return it to Mrs. Larson." I pull the sweater over my head and hand it to Michael. The sweater was warm and the air is cool, and my skin breaks out into ripples of goosebumps in protest. "Thanks for lending it to me."

"No problem." Michael is standing directly in front of me, Mrs. Larson's pink sweater balled up inside-out in his hands. His bangs are in need of a trim and keep falling into his eyes. He looks a little overwhelmed, which isn't surprising. If you're not used to the drama of being a Delaney it can be pretty exhausting. Still, he helped me search for Suzy and sat through Denise's lectures on cuticle care and was there for one of the most important nights of my life. Maybe it's this, or finding Suzy, or my mom being cancer-free, or some powerful combination of all three, but right now, at this moment, I am overcome with something that feels like love for wonderful, dependable, floppy-haired Michael Greenblat.

And so I close the distance between us and kiss him. Right there in Doug's driveway. Our noses bump and I don't know where to put my hands, but it doesn't matter because we're kissing and it's soft and warm and tastes like root beer. Mrs. Larson's sweater is squished between us, otherwise I would wrap my arms around him because I want to know what his back feels like and bury my hands in his hair and find out if it's as soft as it looks. A second or maybe a year passes and I pull away because if I don't, I'm afraid I'll forget to breathe. Michael still has his eyes closed and he looks as flushed as I feel.

The screen door squeaks, bangs, and suddenly Doug is back. "All right, Mikey, let's get you home."

The spell is broken. Silently, Michael and I float back to the car and file in, me in the front, and him in the back. I don't say a word all the way to Michael's house. I'm afraid that if I speak I'll lose the feeling of the kiss on my lips, which are still tingling.

Michael gives Doug directions and thanks him for the ride when he gets out of the car.

"No problem-o, Michael! Thanks for helping Clarissa search for Suzy."

Michael blushes at the mention of my name. "No problem," he says, looking straight at me.

I watch him as he walks up to his front door, looking back once over his shoulder and raising his hand in a dorky little wave. I look away, some of the magic rubbing off and embarrassment taking its place. Did anybody see us? Can Doug tell? Was I too forward? Does Michael think I'm a good kisser? I do my best to wash away all bad thoughts and hold onto the memory of the kiss, which is already fleeting. Why is it so hard to remember good things?

Doug sighs. "Well, Clarissa, I'm beat. This has been a day for the history books." He can say that again.

News

It isn't until later, in bed, that I realize Benji doesn't know yet. I was so worried and then surprised and then happy and then, well, *kissing* that I didn't even think about calling him until right now.

I slip out of bed and tiptoe as quietly as I can to the kitchen, where I take the phone off its cradle and bring it back to bed with me. This isn't the kind of news you can hold off on sharing until the next day. I burrow into the sheets and dial the numbers I've known by heart as long as I care to remember, praying the Dentonator doesn't pick up.

"Hello?" He may sound sleepy, but I'd recognize Benji's voice anywhere.

"Did I wake you up?"

"Clarissa?"

"Obviously."

"It's really late."

"I know, but I couldn't wait to tell you."

"Tell me what?"

I pause for effect. "My mom is officially cancer-free."

"She is? For real?"

"For real."

"I can't believe it."

"Believe it."

"It's too good to be true. I'm going to wake up tomorrow and think I dreamed the whole thing."

"Since when have you carried on whole conversations in your sleep?"

"Never," he admits.

"Maybe you should write it down," I suggest. "Annie Delaney has been declared free of cancer." I love saying it out loud.

"I could have written that in my sleep."

"Maybe you should add 'this is not a dream.' That doesn't seem like something a sleepwalker would write."

"I can't find a pen."

"You won't think it's a dream, Benji. And if you do, you can call me first thing and I'll tell you again."

"Even if it's early?"

"Even if it's early."

"I'm so relieved."

"Me, too."

"Relieved doesn't even begin to explain how relieved I feel."

"I know. Me, too."

We lapse into silence. I don't know what Benji's thinking, maybe he's fallen asleep, but I'm thinking about all the words I know and how I can't think of a single one that expresses how I feel right now. For a second I consider telling him about the kiss, but I'm not ready to share that yet. I want to keep it to myself, if only for one night. "Are you still awake?"

"I think so."

"I'll let you get back to sleep. I just had to tell you."

"No, I'm glad you called. I'm so happy for you and your mom."

"Thanks."

"Goodnight, Clarissa."

"Goodnight, Benji."

The weight of the day has finally worn me down and I can't imagine walking all the way back to the kitchen to return the phone to its cradle. I intend to set it on my nightstand but I am too overcome with sleepiness. Instead, I fall asleep holding it tucked under my arm.

That night I sleep better than I have in more than a year.

Nice

The next morning, Doug is sitting at my kitchen table eating cereal. It's nine o'clock. Does that mean Doug was here all night, or did he just arrive this morning? I'm not sure I want to know the answer to that question. One thing's for sure; I'm glad I changed out of my penguin pyjamas and into real clothes. I clear my throat.

Doug looks up from the paper and smiles his tractor beam smile; it's very hard not to get drawn in by a smile like that. "Isn't it a beautiful morning?" He shakes the cereal box. "Froot Loops?"

I grab a bowl from the cupboard and pull up the chair opposite Doug. He's busy frowning at the crossword, which gives me a chance to scrutinize him unnoticed. The air smells faintly of shaving cream, and not the raspberry-scented stuff my mom uses. This is a sharper, cleaner scent; it's coming from Doug, who looks freshly shaved. Plus his hair is still damp at the edges. Did he shower here, or at home?

"I didn't think a health nut like you would eat Froot Loops," I say lightly.

"Some things are hard to resist," Doug says. "Besides, I live by an eighty-five percent philosophy."

"What does that mean?"

"It means I eat well eighty-five percent of the time. That way I'm allowed to break the rules now and then."

"Is that what you teach your clients? To only give eighty-five percent to everything they do?" I ask.

"Yes and no. Yes, I tell my clients to eat healthy eighty-five percent of the time, and no, I don't expect them to give anything but their best when it comes to effort."

"That seems contradictory," I point out.

Doug winks at me. "Good thing you're not my client. I think you'd give me a run for my money."

We lapse into silence, concentrating on our breakfasts. The only sound is the crunching of Froot Loops, the scrape of spoon against bowl, and Doug tapping the edge of his pen against the table. Every once in a while he hums aloud and the pen becomes a drumstick, tapping out a rhythm that only Doug can hear. I can't stand not knowing anymore.

"Where's my mother?" I blurt.

"She's still in bed. I thought I'd let her sleep in for a bit." When I don't answer, Doug looks up from his paper. "I just dropped by from an early-bird session at the gym," he explains. "I brought her a smoothie."

The elastic bands that have been stretched tight around my chest expand and relax and I feel like I can breathe deeply again. "Oh, that's nice," I say weakly.

Doug smiles. "I'm a nice guy. I would have brought you something but I don't know what you like."

"That's okay," I say.

"Say, can you help me out here?" Doug asks. "I'm stuck."

"What are you stuck on?" I ask.

"Twenty-three down, a four-letter word for friend."

"Chum?"

"Nope, tried that."

"Mate?"

"Ooh, very Australian, but no."

"Ally?"

Doug grins. "Jackpot! I knew I could count on you." He does a little drum roll against the paper and hits an imaginary cymbal above my head.

"For the record," I say, "my favourite smoothie is strawberry; just strawberry, no banana."

Doug winks. "Gotcha."

Week

"If you're going with Michael, should I call Andrew?"

"I'm not going *with* Michael, we're all going together."

Mattie rolls her eyes. "I know, but everyone is paired up but me. You and Michael, your mom and Doug —"

"Denise isn't with anyone," I point out. "Besides, we're not sitting with them, anyways. Can you imagine?" I trail off, letting Mattie picture Denise and Doug at a play, all that laughing and thigh-slapping and whistling like they're at a ball game or the rodeo.

Mattie sighs. "Fine. But Andrew is cute, right?"

I shrug. "I don't know, I never noticed."

"Well, notice! I know you only have eyes for Michael, but just this once, for me, look at Andrew Kane and tell me if you think he's cute."

Andrew Kane is Mattie's newest crush. He's pretty quiet, really good at math, and has a lot of red hair.

"He looks like a long-lost Weasley brother," I say.

"I happen to like red hair. It stands out."

"I didn't say I didn't like it."

"Clarissa, be serious!" Mattie begs.

"I don't know much about him," I admit. "He doesn't say much."

"I know, he's a man of mystery!" Mattie gushes. "Plus he would never hang out with Josh and those guys from the skate park. I can't believe I ever liked Josh. Or Declan! Oh, please don't tell anyone about that, I'm so embarrassed." Mattie shakes her head, as if she can physically get rid of the three weeks she was in love with Declan. "Anyway. Do you think Andrew is the kind of boy who likes going to the theatre?"

"It's just a community production, it's not like you're taking him to the opera," I remind her.

"Maybe Michael can ask him! And then it would be like a group thing, which is way less intimidating. And at the show, you can sit with Michael and I can sit with Andrew . . ."

The wheels in Mattie's head are turning too fast for me. As she talks through her plan of attack, I let my gaze wander. It inevitably lands on Michael, who is sitting with some guys from the basketball team, laughing away, like nothing ever happened.

I will him to look up at me. It's been four days since that night in Doug's driveway and we haven't spoken since. I thought about calling him, but shouldn't he be the one doing the calling? *I* kissed him, after all.

"Hello? Earth to Clarissa," Mattie is waving her hand in front of my eyes.

"Yes, you should definitely invite Andrew," I say.

Mattie rolls her eyes. "I know, I already told you that. I knew you weren't listening. You're thinking about Michael again, I can tell. You have that look on your face."

"What look? I don't have a look."

"You do," Mattie insists. Then her face softens. "So he still hasn't called you?"

I shake my head. "No."

"Men!" I thought we had discussed the whole kiss thing to death a few days ago, when I first told her, but Mattie still has her theories. "Maybe he's waiting for you to call. After all, you were the aggressor —"

"Aggressor? It's not like I *forced* him to kiss me!"

"Of course not! I just meant you were the brave one. It's not a bad thing, but maybe since you were the one who made the first move, he's waiting for you to make the second one, too."

"What happened to your whole 'the ball is in his court' theory?"

Mattie shrugs. "I don't know. Maybe he thinks it's too soon to make a move?"

"It's been four days!"

"I know that, and you know that, but Michael is a boy. We can't ever really know what he's thinking."

I snort. "Well, that's reassuring."

Mattie gets all dreamy-eyed. "At least you were kissed."

"Correction, *he* was kissed. I was the one doing the kissing."

We go back to eating our lunches in silence. I'm so agitated I can barely sit still. What is happening to me? I used to be a normal person who was able to carry on a normal conversation, and now all I can think about is Michael and why he isn't calling me. If this is love, I want no part of it. It's so much easier to not like anyone.

"Sorry I'm late." Benji shows up at the table and slides his cafeteria tray next to mine.

"Lunchtime is practically over," I say. "Where have you been?"

"I had a costume fitting," he explains. "Wait till you see the headpiece I get to wear. It was rented from a theatre company in Toronto. The curls are made from real hair."

Mattie claps her hands. "That is so exciting, I can't wait to see it! Three more sleeps!"

"Real hair? Isn't that kind of creepy?" I ask.

"A wig is made from real hair," Benji points out. He looks back and forth at us. "So, what did I miss? What were you guys talking about?"

"Andrew Kane," I blurt out, before Mattie can say anything. "Mattie thinks he's cute."

"But he never says anything," Benji says.

"So? He's probably thinking deep thoughts. He's probably the smartest kid in our class," Mattie says.

"She's thinking of asking him to come see your show with us," I add.

Mattie launches into her list of reasons why Andrew Kane is better than Josh. She doesn't mention Declan. I am grateful that she can take a hint. I haven't told Benji about the kiss yet, partly because I don't want to do or say anything to distract him before his show opens, since he's already a big bundle of nerves, and also because I'm not sure how to bring it up. It might make things weird between us.

"You should definitely ask him," Benji concludes. "Do it now!"

We all swivel in our chairs to look at Andrew, sitting at the corner table eating his lunch with a book open beside him. "What do you think he's reading?" Benji asks.

"It looks thick," Mattie observes. "I bet it's something dark and brooding and serious."

"It's probably his math textbook," I point out.

Benji giggles. "How are you going to ask him?"

Mattie frowns. "I don't know yet."

"You should send him a note," I suggest. "You plus me plus *The Wizard of Oz* equals one hot date." Benji laughs out loud and Mattie squeals, smacking me on the arm. "Or you could just give him your number. We know he's good with those," I add.

"You're horrible," she says, but she's smiling as she says it.

"Are you going with Michael?" Benji asks.

I stop laughing. "Well he's sitting *with* us, if that's what you mean," I say. Try as I might, I can't keep the stiffness out of my voice.

"*With* is such a vague term," Mattie muses.

Benji looks from me to Mattie and back to me again. His forehead wrinkles but he doesn't say anything more about it. I can tell he's hurt, though. He knows there is more to the story than Mattie and I are letting on, but for some reason, we aren't sharing it with him. Pangs of guilt, like a hundred tiny needles, stab me in the gut. I know how it feels to be left out. For a moment, I consider telling him the whole story. But then I'd have to admit that I didn't tell him about the kiss on Saturday night and I don't want to open *that* can of worms, especially with his show only a few days away.

I give Mattie a nudge. "Come on, go ask Andrew. Lunch is almost over."

"So?" she squeals.

I give her an ultimatum: "You have until the end of the day to ask him, or I'm asking him myself."

Mattie's face darkens. I guess the Only if Josh Plays Too birthday party incident is still fresh in her mind. She lets out a long breath. "Fine," she agrees. "But just as friends. With a boy as shy as Andrew you have to go slow. I don't want to scare him off."

"You know, you dating Andrew could work out well for all of us. Just think of how much better our math marks will be!"

Mattie groans and tries to smack me again but I'm too fast for her and I duck just in time. I admit it was kind of a lame joke, but those are the kind that Benji likes best. Sure enough, Benji smiles, but it's not enough to put an end to the guilt eating away at my stomach.

***

Day Six. After two days of complete and utter telephonic silence, the phone rings. I run for it, expecting to hear Michael on the other end of the line.

"Hello?"

"Clarissa! Just the gal I wanted to talk to! Doug here. I was just wondering, is this play the sort of thing you dress up for?"

"I don't think it matters."

"What are you going to wear?"

"I haven't thought about it yet," I say honestly. It depends on whether or not Michael comes. Mattie thinks I should wear skirts more often, but if I'm going to put myself through the torture of wearing a skirt, it better be for a good reason. I guess Michael is a good enough reason.

"Better put your mother on, I'll see what she's wearing and go from there."

"It's not prom, Doug."

"Put her on anyways. I haven't heard her dulcet tones all day."

Barf.

Mom and Doug talk for what feels like an eternity, but it turns out to be only seven minutes. I know because I keep looking at the clock on the DVD player. It would be just my luck that Michael would call while my mom was on the phone. When the gush-fest is over, I keep the phone by my side while I watch television. This way I will be the first to pick it up if it rings again. And sure enough, half an hour later, it does.

"Hello?"

"Minipop? Is that you?"

"Hi, Janine."

"I just heard the news! You must be so thrilled! You know, I've been praying for your mama every night. I got my sister, my husband Gary, my friend Sandy and her husband Eric, Jen from my office, my priest, and a bunch of other people to remember your mama in their prayers and look how things turned out! Even if you're not the religious type, you can't deny the power of positive thought."

"I guess not. Well, thanks, Janine."

"Listen, is your mother there? I wouldn't mind speaking to her myself."

"I think she's with a client," I lie. "Can she call you back?"

"Sure thing, Minipop! I'm just so pleased for the two of you!"

I hang up and hope that a little white lie doesn't undo all that positive energy Janine and company have sent our way. Maybe it is just a bunch of hocus-pocus, but I'm in no position to sneer at any healing methods right now.

When the phone rings again, I think, this is it; third time's the charm.

"Hello?"

"Hello, may I speak to Clarissa, please?"

"Mattie, I can't talk," I say shortly.

"Why not?"

"Because I'm waiting for a phone call!"

"From Michael?"

I bristle at the pity in Mattie's voice. "No!"

"No?"

"Well . . . maybe."

"It's okay, Clarissa. You don't have to be embarrassed. I'd be doing the same thing if I were you."

"Can we talk later?"

"Of course! Call me the second you get off the phone with Michael."

"I will."

"Promise?"

"I said I will, Mattie."

"I'll send you good vibes! Bye!"

But I don't end up calling Mattie later. Why would I, when there is nothing to report? After all that activity, the phone is silent for the rest of the night.

Late

"Is this exciting, or what? I just can't imagine that shy little thing up there in front of all these people, singing and dancing!" We haven't been here five minutes and already I want to kill Denise.

Mattie isn't helping much. "I know!" she gushes. "He can barely put up his hand in class! It's like we're witnessing a transformation right before our eyes!"

I scan the crowds for Michael, who said he would meet us here. My arms are full of flowers, a congratulations card I made myself, and the soundtrack of a musical called *Wicked*, wrapped up in the comics section of yesterday's newspaper. I'd never heard of *Wicked* before, but Charity told him about it and it's all Benji's been talking about for weeks. I couldn't find it anywhere, so Doug helped me order it online.

Everyone is washed and dressed up for the occasion, even Doug. He managed to find a nice shirt and tie to wear. Mom teases him about the tie, making a big show of straightening it and telling him that he cleans up nice.

"I should wear a tie more often," Doug jokes.

I recognize the tie from the day I went rooting around in his closet but I don't say a word.

Mom is wearing a pearl pendant on a chain. It was a gift

from Doug. I'm not really into jewellery, but even I have to admit that it's pretty. It looks like a glossy white raindrop.

"Wow," Mattie whispers. "How much do you think that necklace cost?"

I roll my eyes. "It's not like it's a ring."

Mattie's eyes shine. "If they get married, will you invite me to the wedding?"

"Where's Michael?" Mom asks.

I shrug, but don't make eye contact with her. Doug gives my shoulder a squeeze. "Don't worry, he'll turn up. Mikey is a real stand-up guy, isn't that right, Clarissa?"

I don't really feel like defending him right now, so I pretend not to hear.

Suddenly Mattie digs her nails into my arm. "Look!" she whispers. "It's Andrew!"

"Ouch." I remove my arm from her grasp, rubbing the little white marks left by her nails, which have been filed into talons.

"Andrew! Over here!" Andrew turns at the sound of his name and reddens as soon as he catches sight of Mattie, waving her arms and grinning like a maniac. I can't tell if he's blushing because he actually likes Mattie or if he's embarrassed. Maybe it's a little bit of both. He nods his head curtly, to show that he's seen us, and starts weaving his way through the crowd toward us.

Denise gives Mattie's shoulder a nudge. "What a cutie! Good job, Mattie."

"He really is cute," Mattie giggles. "Look at his pants! I think they're pressed!"

Andrew arrives and Mattie puts on a big show about introducing him to everyone. He really is a nice boy, and a much better choice than Josh or Declan. Mattie can't stop smiling. I'm happy she's finally found a crush who is worthy of her admittedly intense affection. I hope Andrew doesn't scare easily.

The doors have opened and people are starting to file into the theatre. Doug does a quick head count.

"All right, so I've got seven tickets and six people, who are we missing?"

"Just Michael," Mattie says.

"We should probably go in now. Clarissa, why don't you wait out here for Michael and we'll save you a couple of seats," Doug suggests.

"Sure," I say.

Mattie looks concerned. "Do you want me to wait with you?" she asks.

"No, I'm fine. Besides you probably shouldn't leave Andrew alone with everyone else. He looks pretty overwhelmed."

"Well, if you're sure you're okay . . ."

"I am."

Mattie gives me a big hug, nearly squeezing the life out of me. For someone with such little upper body strength, she sure is a powerful hugger. "I'll save you a seat next to me, okay?" she says.

"Great."

And then she hurries into the theatre.

As more and more people arrive, I start to get nervous. The woman taking tickets at the door keeps smiling sympathetically at me. When there is a lull in people, she asks, "Waiting for someone?"

"Obviously," I snap.

She doesn't smile at me again.

Five minutes to go. Where is Michael? I can't believe he

wouldn't show. He promised he would come. He doesn't seem like the kind of person who would say one thing and do another. Even if he is embarrassed about the whole kissing fiasco (it still hurts to think of it as a fiasco — how can something be so important to one person and mean nothing to another?) this isn't about me, it's about Benji. It's like Mattie says, Michael is one of us; when he decided to help bring Terry DiCarlo down last year, he was making a silent pact with us. We were more than friends; we were partners in crime, protectors of the innocent, defenders of justice. He risked detention and possible bodily harm for Benji last year, the least he could do is show up for his play.

"You should probably go take your seat," the woman at the door says. "Does your friend have a ticket already?"

"No, I bought it for him."

"I'm not allowed to let latecomers in during the scenes," she says. "But if you want to leave it here with me, I can sneak him in during the applause."

I feel bad for snapping at her before. "That would be nice, thanks."

"What's his name?" she asks.

"Michael. Michael Greenblat."

Two minutes to go and the door swings open. The woman smiles brightly. "Right under the wire, is this your friend?"

But it's not Michael.

Star

The Dentonator nods at me. "Clarissa," he says.

"You're late," I point out.

"Yeah, I had to change at work. Wasn't sure if I was going to make it."

I look at his shirt, buttoned up to the neck and tucked into his jeans, and I can't remember the last time I saw Benji's dad in anything but a t-shirt.

The lights flick off and on.

"The show's about to start," the woman at the door says.

The Dentonator takes off his ball cap and runs his fingers through his hat hair. "Do you mind if I sit with you?"

"Sure, my mom is saving us seats."

***

The show is wonderful. It's so good, I almost forget that it's supposed to be Michael sitting beside me, not the Dentonator. Charity, of course, is amazing. Her trademark mane is hidden under a dark wig, plaited into Dorothy's signature braids. After a while, I forget that I'm watching Charity and I start to think of her only as Dorothy. Everyone is great, but she has an extra something that makes her stand out. I guess that's what they call star quality.

210

Benji doesn't come on stage until halfway through the first act. I know the story by heart, so after the scene with the Tin Man, I start to get nervous for him. I guess Mattie does, too, because she grabs my hand and holds on tight. On my other side, the Dentonator shifts in his seat. Is it my imagination, or is he leaning forward a little?

And then there he is. I smile the whole time he's on stage — I can't help it, he's that good! He speaks louder than I've ever heard him speak before, and his Cowardly Lion stutter is spot on. He doesn't sound nervous at all; he sounds perfect.

As the lights go down, the audience laughs and cheers. My entire row, the whole rowdy gang of us, is the first to jump up and give a standing ovation. I want to shout, that's my best friend, that's my Benji! But instead, I clap along with the audience, practically bursting with pride.

***

After the show, we wait in the lobby for the actors to exit the dressing rooms. There are lots of people around, holding flowers and smiling and laughing about the show.

Denise is practically beside herself with glee. "Well son of a gun, can you believe it? I just can't believe it! He was amazing, wasn't he? He truly was amazing! I never would have guessed."

One by one, the actors emerge, wearing regular clothes, but still in their heavy stage makeup. The girls wear false eyelashes and lots of blue eye shadow. The boys' faces have been mostly wiped clean, but you can still see a shadow of eyeliner around their eyes and traces of red lipstick on their lips. They smile bashfully as people cheer and shower them with applause and hugs. There is a loud cheer when

Charity emerges, looking tired but happy, her magnificent hair flattened on top from her wig. She catches my eye and gives me a little wave before being swallowed by a group of adoring fans.

The Dentonator actually looks uncomfortable, for once in his life. He keeps shifting his weight from side to side, looking at the clock, at the door, and then at us. Maybe it's because he's wearing a collared shirt.

"Do you have to be somewhere?" I ask pointedly.

"I didn't know I was supposed to bring flowers," he says, gazing at the hordes of people bearing large bouquets. I wish I could take back my tone. I feel sorry for him. How was he supposed to know? It's not like anyone gave him flowers after a big hockey game. As far as I know, this is the first time the Dentonator has ever stepped foot inside a theatre.

I hand him my bouquet. "Here," I say, "you can take these."

"No, I couldn't. You bought them so you should give them to him."

"It's okay, I have something else for him, too."

But the Dentonator shakes his head. "It wouldn't be right."

"I think I saw a woman selling roses by the concession stand at intermission," Mom says gently. "I'm sure she has some left over."

The Dentonator looks relieved. "Thanks, Annie. I'll go check that out."

When Benji slips out, for once I am happy to be with such a rowdy group of people. Charity may have prompted lots of cheering, but it's nothing compared to the welcome that Benji receives. Denise puts two fingers in her mouth and whistles, and Doug says, "Hey, look, it's the Cowardly Lion!" Strangers step forward to clap Benji on the back and say congratulations as he makes his way over to his cheering section. Even under all that foundation, I can see that he's turned a deep shade of pink.

"You were truly wonderful," Mom says warmly.

Doug holds out his hand for a shake. "Bang-up job, Benjamin."

Benji's father steps forward, thrusting an armload of individually wrapped roses toward Benji. There must be at least a dozen of them in all colours: red, yellow, pink, and white.

"For me?" Benji says.

The Dentonator nods. "That was really something. I never could have got up there in front of all those people," he says.

I roll my eyes, but by the way Benji grins I can tell he doesn't think it was a lame thing to say.

"Would you look at that," Denise whispers. "He must have bought up every last one of those roses."

"He has a good heart," Mom says.

Denise gets a familiar sparkle in her eye. "You know, he is still in good shape for a man his age."

Mom laughs. I've heard about as much as I can handle. I break away from the group and make my way toward the star, withering under the weight of all his flowers.

"Need a hand with all those flowers?" I ask. Benji hands me a bouquet, but keeps clutching the dozen or so single roses from his dad. "I got something for you, too, but I'll give it to you later. It looks like you've got your hands full anyway."

"You didn't have to," Benji protests.

"Don't be stupid, I wanted to!" I insist.

"What did you think? Honestly?"

"Honestly? It was amazing. You were amazing. Don't tell me you didn't hear all those people cheering for you."

Benji grins. "I totally did. Are you coming out with us?"

"Where are you going?"

"Most of the cast is going to the Dairy Bar for ice cream. It's tradition."

"I wouldn't want to be in the way. It sounds like it's a cast thing."

"I want you to come. Mattie and Andrew can come, too. Please, Clarissa? You haven't come to anything yet."

"Okay. But only because you're a star."

Mess

The Dairy Bar is at full capacity. Outside, people sprawl across the picnic tables and run back and forth from the pickup window carrying ice cream cones in both hands. It's the first night that feels like summer is right around the corner. The unexpected heat is making people giddy. And flirty. I feel like I'm in the middle of some teenage mating ritual.

Inside, the Dairy Bar is full of actors and their friends. It is the perfect after-show hangout for theatre types: loud, fun, and campy. All of the employees wear pointed paper caps that look like they may have been children's sailing boats in another life. The radio is tuned to the oldies station and at every booth there is a shrine to someone famous and long-dead: James Dean, Marilyn Monroe, Elvis Presley. Mattie, Andrew, Benji, and I stuff ourselves into the *I Love Lucy* booth.

Mattie grabs the menu, personalized with all sorts of *I Love Lucy* facts, and reads aloud. "Did you know seven out of every ten people with televisions watched the episode where Lucy gives birth to Little Ricky?"

"Gross! Can't you read the specials?"

"It's not like they showed the actual process of birth," Mattie protests.

I shudder and cover my ears.

"All right, all right! Oh, look! Onion rings are half price! I love onion rings, only I can never finish an entire basket . . ." Mattie trails off, smiling sweetly at Andrew.

"Do you want to share a basket?" he asks. That Andrew is much quicker on the uptake than Josh Simmons.

Mattie's smile goes from bright to megawatt. "I would *love* to!"

It occurs to me that this is where my dad took my mom on their first date. I wonder which booth they sat in. Probably James Dean. The tortured-poetic types (or the type that pretends to be a tortured poet) would probably pick James Dean. Doug would never pick James Dean. He'd pick something goofy. In fact, he'd probably sit right here, in the *I Love Lucy* booth. I hate to admit it, but these days I am on Team Doug. Sorry, Bill. DNA isn't everything.

"Do you want to split something?" Benji asks me.

"No way, I can eat an entire basket to myself and then some. Besides, I think I want ice cream."

"Hey, look, it's The Benj!" Beckett enters the Dairy Bar, followed closely by Mika and some other girls I don't recognize. One of them can't keep her arms off him, and the other keeps smiling with her mouth closed. As they get closer I can see the glint of braces in her mouth. They must have been in the play, because I can still see smudges of eyeliner and streaks of orange foundation on their necks. Mika has her arm flung around Beckett's shoulder and is gazing adoringly at his face. Beckett doesn't seem to notice.

Somehow, all four of them end up squeezing into our booth. Mattie is pressed right up against Andrew, who blushes and pretends to be studying the menu.

Soon fries and onion rings arrive in red plastic baskets,

lined in white newsprint. Beckett makes a big show of smacking his lips and licking each vinegar-stained finger. "Magnifico!" he says.

"What's that, Spanish?" Mika asks.

Cripes.

"So what did you guys think of the show?" Braces asks. "Tell the truth."

"It was amazing," Mattie says. "I loved every second of it."

"Hard to believe it was The Benj's first show," Beckett says, giving him a playful punch on the arm. "He's a natural."

Benji winces, rubbing his arm, but he can't help but smile at the same time. "Thanks."

"The first of many, right, little bro?" Beckett holds his hand out for a high-five, which Benji reluctantly gives him.

"I hope so," Benji says earnestly, making the girls laugh.

"You are just the cutest thing," says Octopus Arms, reaching out and pinching Benji's cheek. "Isn't he the cutest thing?"

Mattie sniffs and her shoulders stiffen. Clearly I'm not the only one who finds these showgirls annoying.

"If by cute you mean talented, then yes," I say coldly.

"Who is this chick?" Braces asks.

"My name is Clarissa Louise Delaney," I say evenly.

"Oooh, is this your girlfriend, Benji?" Braces teases.

"I hope not," says Octopus Arms, removing her tentacles from Beckett and draping her arm around Benji's shoulders. "This one is good boyfriend material."

Benji turns almost as red as the ketchup on the table and squirms under Octopus Arms' tentacle. "Excuse me, I need to go to the bathroom," he says.

Beckett cups his hands around his mouth and adopts a corny radio announcer's voice. "Ladies and Gents, The

Benj!" Mika and the other girls laugh as Benji scurries toward the bathroom, head down, cheeks burning.

Once he's safely out of earshot, Braces leans across the table. "No, seriously. So what's the deal? Are you guys together?"

"No, we are not together," I say. I have to speak slowly and carefully to keep from exploding.

"Clarissa's already taken," Mattie chimes in. Everyone is surprised, but no one more than me.

"Really?" Andrew asks, frowning.

Mattie panics. "Well, in her heart anyway," she says uncertainly.

Octopus Arms and Braces lean forward expectantly. "Sounds like there's a story there," says Braces.

Mattie busies herself by stuffing what's left of the onion rings into her mouth and avoiding eye contact. So much for her "don't eat like a pig in front of boys" philosophy.

"No story," I say quickly. Perhaps a little too quickly, because Braces and Octopus Arms share a knowing glance and then turn all sympathetic.

"Boys suck," Braces says.

"Really suck," Octopus Arms agrees.

"Hey!" Beckett protests. "I'm sitting right here!"

"You're not a boy, you're a man," Mika giggles.

Barf. If this is what high school is like, I'll stay back a year, thank you very much.

"It's okay, she's just upset," Mattie explains to the rest of the table.

"I am not upset," I insist through gritted teeth.

"Let it all out, Clarissa. It's healthy to let your feelings out," Braces says.

"Let what out? What's the matter?" A hush falls over the

table as Benji slides back into his seat, looking at me with concern. When no one offers an explanation, he asks again. "Clarissa? What are you upset about?"

I try to blow it off. "Nothing, Benji, don't worry about it."

But Mattie isn't having any of it. "It's Michael," she confesses. "You know, in a million years I never would have thought that he of all people would treat a girl like this. He seems so respectful."

Now Benji looks truly alarmed. "Treat a girl like what? What's going on?"

"He still hasn't called her."

"So?"

"So? A whole week is a long time not to call someone after you've kissed them."

Benji's mouth drops open. "You KISSED him?"

Braces lifts her hand for a high-five. "All right! Nicely done, Clarissa!"

I send her a glare powerful enough that she drops her hand and looks sheepish. "Yes, I kissed Michael, and he hasn't talked to me since. Can we please move on?"

Benji is crestfallen. "I can't believe you didn't tell me."

"Well, obviously nothing came of it, so there was nothing to tell."

Mika shakes her head. "Boys," she says. Octopus Arms and Braces nod with her.

"Oh, Clarissa. I'm so, so sorry," Benji says. He looks so sad I want to punch him.

"Don't be sorry for me! I don't care! It didn't mean anything. It was a spur of the moment kind of thing. I lost Suzy and then I got the news about my mom and then we found Suzy again, and it just happened. I would have kissed anybody who was there, I would have kissed *him*!" In my panicked state, I point wildly at Beckett who, for once, is at a loss for words.

Mika gives me the stink-eye and puts a protective hand on Beckett's arm, who finds his voice again.

"Whoa, Clarissa, you're nice and everything, but I think you're a little young for me —"

"Cripes, I didn't mean I'd *actually* do it. It was just an example! As if I'd want to kiss you."

Braces frowns and says, "Whoa, Clarissa, that was harsh."

"Listen, Basket —"

"It's Beckett —"

"I don't care what your stupid name is. You don't know anything about me, so just back off."

"And I thought Charity was a drama queen," Octopus Arms mutters under her breath.

To my surprise, I find myself defending Charity. "Hey! Leave Charity out of this!"

"Aren't we touchy," Braces says primly.

I want to rip the braces right off her teeth. "I am not touchy and I am not mad about Michael. I don't care about Michael Greenblat. I'm sorry I ever kissed him and I'm sorry I ever told anyone about it! So please stop putting words into my mouth and believe me when I say, once and for all, that Michael Greenblat is as good as dead to me!"

I turn on my heel, ready to make a grand exit worthy of the stage — the kind people will be talking about for months to come — only to see Michael loitering near the cash register, staring at me like I'm some kind of horrible, heartless person.

Which, of course, at least in this instant, I am.

Over

"Michael? Michael!" I push my way through the crowds but am not fast enough to catch up to Michael, who has slipped out the front door and into the night. I sit on an empty picnic table bench, feeling about as low as low can be. A bell jingles and Mattie exits the Dairy Bar, smilingly sadly at me.

"Well, that's the end of that," I sigh.

"Maybe not," Mattie says, but I can tell that she doesn't believe it.

"Well, I might as well go home. I don't want to ruin anyone else's night."

"That's probably a good idea," Mattie agrees.

"Let's go."

Mattie hesitates, twirling a thick chunk of hair around her finger. "Actually, Andrew asked if he could walk me home. Do you mind?"

"Of course not! Go, go! I'll be fine."

Mattie looks intensely relieved. "Oh, thank you! I hope you don't feel abandoned. It's not that I value boys over our friendship. It's just, well, he's going to walk me home!"

"It's fine."

"Are you sure? Because if you want me to, I can go with you. Sisters before misters and all that."

"It's fine, Mattie, really."

Mattie gives me a quick hug. "I'll call you when I get home and tell you everything, I promise!" Mattie runs back into the Dairy Bar to retrieve her purse and her date, just missing Benji who approaches me like you would a wild animal — slowly, and with caution.

"Are you heading home?" he asks.

I nod. "I don't want to cause any more damage."

"I'll come with you."

***

We walk in silence before Benji clears his throat and says, "Well, that was something."

"I'm sorry I ruined your party."

"You didn't ruin it," Benji says. "Actually, you were kind of the life of the party. People will be talking about this for ages."

"Oh, great!" I moan. "I've really done it this time, haven't I?"

Benji nods grimly. "I'll say. The truth is, Clarissa, whether you want to admit it or not, you're very good at causing drama."

"But I don't mean to!" I wail.

Benji pats my shoulder. "I know." He pauses, then asks, "Why didn't you tell me about Michael?"

"You mean about the —"

Benji blushes and cuts me off. "Yeah, about the . . ."

"See? You can't even say it! How could I tell you about it knowing it would make you so uncomfortable!"

"I thought we were best friends."

"We are!" I take a breath and try to explain it to him. "It all happened so fast. We had just found out that my mom's cancer was all gone, and you were so busy with the show and your new friends, and I guess I just didn't think you'd be interested."

Benji stops dead in his tracks and stares at me in disbelief. "Of course I'd be interested!"

"I thought maybe you'd think I was trying to steal your thunder or something,"

Benji frowns. "Steal your thunder?" he repeats.

I wave him off. "It's something Mattie says. Anyway, I'm sorry. I promise I'll tell you about any future kissing. Not that it will be happening any time soon," I add wryly.

Benji grimaces. "No, I guess not."

"What do I do now?" I ask, dreading the answer.

"You have to go apologize to Michael."

I sigh. "I feel like all I do these days is apologize for all the stupid things I've been doing lately." I look to Benji for strength. "This is going to be hard."

"Really hard," Benji adds.

"What do I say?"

"I don't know," Benji admits, "but I'm glad I'm not you right now."

"Gee, thanks."

"You're welcome."

Wish

It takes me a full day to work up the courage to go over and apologize to Michael. I spend most of it pacing around the house until my mom hollers at me from the Hair Emporium, where she's giving it a good clean.

"You're wearing down the carpet," she complains. "Are you going to tell me about it or do I have to get my scissors out again?"

I know she's joking, but I run my hand through my slightly too-short hair and laugh nervously. I trudge downstairs and flop into one of the big, red chairs. "I have to apologize to someone," I admit.

"Who?" she asks.

"Michael."

To her credit, Mom only nods, as if it's normal that we're talking about a boy who is not Benji. "What did you do?" she asks, a smile playing at the corners of her lips. "Hit him with a badminton racquet?"

"I wish," I say. "I said some horrible things about him in front of a group of people. I didn't know he was there. Not that that makes any difference."

Mom's eyebrows go up but she continues scrubbing. "A group of people?" she repeats.

"Well, a restaurant full of friends and strangers," I clarify.

224

"Ouch," Mom says. "Sounds like apologizing is the right thing to do."

"Doesn't make it any easier."

"Of course not. If apologizing were easy, we'd have achieved world peace ages ago."

I smile in spite of myself. "Is that what you wished for when you won the Dairy Queen pageant?"

Mom laughs. "God, no, that's way too Miss America. I wished for tax relief for farmers."

"Really?"

"Well, the pageant was sponsored by the dairy farmers of Ontario."

"Still, that's a little obvious, isn't it?"

Mom shrugs. "I just played the game by their rules, made everyone feel good about themselves and the work that they do. I don't see what's wrong with that. Besides, a true wish is something private. Definitely not something you share with a panel of judges."

"Have you ever had a wish come true?" I ask.

Mom smiles. "Twice. First with you and now —"

"— with Doug," I finish.

"Bingo."

It's now or never. I take a deep breath and let the first of many things that have been weighing me down off my chest. "I snooped in his closet, when I went to feed Suzy."

Mom puts down the sponge she's been using to scour the sinks in the Hair Emporium. She doesn't say a word, just stares at me expectantly.

"I didn't find anything, though. No skeletons, no dirty laundry."

"I could have told you that without you looking through his private things."

"I wanted to be sure. Are you going to tell him?"

Mom thinks hard before responding, "You left a chair out."

"What?"

"In the bedroom, you left a chair out."

Of course, the kitchen chair. Some detective I turned out to be. My heart sinks all the way to the bottom of my toes.

"So he knows?"

Mom nods.

"How come he didn't say anything?"

"I don't know. Maybe he didn't want to embarrass you."

I didn't think it was possible to feel any worse, but I do. The guy whose house I got caught snooping in didn't want to make *me* feel bad.

"What should I do?"

"You could apologize."

I sigh. "I'm getting really good at it," I say.

Mom laughs. "Thank you for telling me. I know you've been keeping things from me lately."

"It's only because I didn't want you to worry over nothing," I protest.

Mom looks hurt. "Your life is not nothing to me," she says.

"I thought if you had more to worry about, you wouldn't be able to concentrate on getting better."

For a second I worry that Mom might burst into tears, but she breathes deeply through her nose and manages to pull herself together. "I am sorry you have had to go through all this, Clarissa. In a perfect world no child would have to deal with a sick parent. But I'm not sick anymore, and you need to start telling me things. I am your mother. I will always worry a little. Not telling me things makes it worse, not better."

"Okay."

Mom smiles, tucking my hair behind my ears with her fingers. It's such a nice gesture I don't even mind that she's still wearing the yellow rubber gloves she cleans in. "Let's start again. This is the first day of us telling each other things, no matter how big or small. Okay?"

"Okay. Does this mean I have to hear about Doug's bad breath or his athlete's foot?"

Mom laughs. "No one wants to hear about that. Now what are the chances I can get you to stick around and help me clean the hair out of the drains? I know how much you love cleaning."

"You wish."

Cool

I've never been to Michael's house before. I pause on the front step before ringing the doorbell. Inside, it sounds like there's a party going on. Or maybe it's a riot. Whatever it is, there's lots of shouting and barking.

The door flies open before I get a chance to knock. A little boy stares at me. "You're not the pizza guy," he says accusingly.

"No."

From inside, a woman yells "David! Who's at the door?"

The boy — David, I assume — yells back. "It's a girl!"

"Well give the girl some money and grab the pizza!"

"She doesn't have a pizza!"

"What?" Someone comes banging down the stairs and then a woman appears in the doorway. Her hair has been hastily tied back and there are soap suds on her hands, which probably has something to do with the very wet, very naked toddler she's holding against her chest.

"Oh. We thought you were the pizza guy," she says. "Can I help you?" Just then a basketball bounces down the hallway, chased by a puppy with enormous paws. "Michael!" she yells. "I asked you to put that ball away. Now the dog's got it. Oh for goodness sakes. Here, can you hold him?"

The woman shoves the toddler into my arms and I am stranded there holding him as she runs after the dog, which is still running after the basketball, with David trailing behind her laughing. The kid is heavy and slippery and is getting the front of my shirt all wet. He twists around to look at me and frowns, placing a wet chubby hand on my cheek. I've never held a baby before; I've never even babysat for walking, talking children. Now he's exploring my face with his hand, trying to find a feature that looks familiar. I shift his weight and he slips a little and grabs onto my shirt with impressive strength. What if I drop him?

"Clarissa?" Michael looks down at me from the top of the stairs.

"Can you help?" I ask, just as the kid starts to whimper. By the time Michael makes it down the stairs the kid is wailing directly into my right ear.

"Shhh, Theo, it's okay." Michael takes the baby, props him over his shoulder and rubs his little back like it's the most natural thing in the world. Theo stops crying and makes gurgling noises, which sounds like he's either happy or is about to throw up. Michael smiles his apologetic, lop-sided smile. "Sorry about that. Welcome to the zoo!"

***

Within five minutes, I have met each of Michael's three brothers. Theo, the wet baby, is eighteen months old; David is five; and Solly, who insists on wearing 3-D glasses, is eight. "Almost nine," he insists. Rambo, the dog, runs through the living room, a running shoe dangling from his jaws.

"Is it always like this?" I ask.

Michael shrugs. "Pretty much."

And I thought life at my house could get a little noisy.

"So, um, can I help you with something?" Michael asks. He can barely look at me, and I don't blame him, after the way I treated him.

"I wanted to talk to you. Actually, I wanted to apologize."

Michael looks over his shoulder and yells up at his mom. "Mom? Is it okay if we go for a walk?"

Michael's mom appears at the top of the stairs. "Well, sure. But don't be too long, you're grounded, remember."

"I remember," Michael mumbles. To me, he says, "Let's go."

***

"Where do you want to go?" Michael asks.

I consider going to the Dairy Bar, but that would be too much like returning to the scene of the crime. Going to the park at St. Paddy's would be cruel, since that's where we were the night of our first (and probably last) kiss, and so I decide to play it safe and suggest the most neutral place I can think of.

"I don't know, maybe the 7-Eleven? We could get slushies."

"Sure," Michael agrees.

The walk there is painfully quiet; it seems neither of us can think of anything to say. After an excruciating three blocks, Michael asks, "So, how was the play?"

"It was great! Benji was great," I say.

"I think I'm going to see it Sunday afternoon. There's a two o'clock show. I was going to go on Friday but I was grounded."

"How come?"

"Well, because of what happened last Friday." Last Friday. The day Suzy went missing. Remission day. The day of our first (and probably last) kiss. "Once we got to your place,

230

I got swept up in everything and forgot to call home. I was an hour and a half late for curfew, so I was grounded. No going out, no internet, no phone."

Everything clicks into place. All the pieces of the puzzle make sense now: why he didn't call me; why he didn't show up at the play. All I can think to say is, "Oh."

"I wanted to call you, but, you know, I couldn't."

"You could have told me at school," I point out.

"I thought about it, but you're always with Mattie or Benji or someone," Michael says. "Plus you seemed kind of mad this week."

I can't help myself, I laugh out loud at this. Michael frowns. "What's so funny?"

"I was mad because you didn't call," I admit.

Michael looks sheepish. "I guess that makes sense. I'd be mad, too."

At 7-Eleven I offer to buy Michael's slushie, just so he knows that there aren't any hard feelings. I throw in some candy and a chocolate bar, too. "Wanna go to the park?"

Michael nods and we make our way back to the skate park, where we sit on the swings stuffing our faces with so much candy we can't possibly be expected to talk to one another.

Once I've had enough and am jittery with sugar, I start my apology. You would think after all the apologizing I've done lately that it would get easier, but it doesn't.

"Look, I'm sorry about what I said at the Dairy Bar. Everyone was getting on my nerves and I just snapped. I didn't mean it and I never would have said it under normal circumstances."

"Normal circumstances" was a term Mattie decided I should use. It felt strange coming out of my mouth, but

Michael doesn't seem to notice, because he shrugs and says, "Okay."

"Okay? Really? So you're fine with . . . everything?"

Michael looks straight at me for the first time. I wonder if he can hear my heart as it skips a beat. "I guess so, as long as you didn't mean it," he says.

"I didn't. And I'm sorry. Really, really, sorry." I hold up a Sour Key. "Truce?"

Michael grabs a Sour Key of his own and touches it with mine. "Truce." Another weight vanishes from my chest. Who knew coming clean could feel so good?

"I should probably head home soon or my mom will get mad," Michael says. We stand to leave. "Unless you wanted to come over? Maybe we could watch a movie?"

My heart is hammering so hard he'd have to be deaf not to hear it. Since I'm on an honesty kick and all, I decide just to go for it. "Is this a date?"

"No." I wonder if he can hear my heart break, because he suddenly looks wary and rushes on, "It's just, after everything, I think I'm through with dating. For a while."

It's surprising how much that hurts. I guess I deserve it. The only thing left to do is put myself on the line. But first, I take a deep breath. "Because if this *was* a date, I'd be okay with that."

The silence that follows is so long that it makes me want to scream, just to put an end to it. What can he possibly be thinking? Mattie says that boys live in a state of perpetual surprise and that I should be patient with them. Unfortunately, being patient is one of the few things that I am not very good at. According to Mattie, girls mature much faster and "you can't blame a boy for being a little slow when it comes to matters of the heart."

"Never mind," I say, just to put Michael out of his misery.

After what feels like a year, Michael manages to say, "Well maybe we could, you know, *not* date for a while and then . . ." But he doesn't finish the sentence. He's looking at me expectantly, like he's waiting for me to fly off the handle. In my head I hear Mattie say "hormones." Oh, no. Have I become one of those girls who pass love notes during class and then cry about boys all lunch hour? Am I Amanda Krespi?

In an effort to look normal, I shrug it off and say, "Yeah, sure, that's what I was thinking," even though I have no idea what I just agreed to. How could I? He never even finished his sentence.

But it seems to do the trick because Michael looks immensely relieved. "Cool," he says.

"Cool," I repeat. Then we both smile at each other until it starts to feel weird and I have to look away. "Michael?"

"Yes?"

"Are you going to — I mean, are we going to — like . . . *not* date other people?"

Michael frowns. "I don't know," he says. "Baseball starts pretty soon. And then there's soccer. I'm going to be pretty busy. I probably won't have time to not date anyone else."

Now it's my turn to feel relieved. "Me neither."

"So do you want to watch a movie?" Michael asks. Then, before I can say anything, he adds, "As friends?"

"Sure, that sounds cool."

"Cool."

Good

"And that's it," I finish.

"What movie did you watch?" Benji asks.

"Some *Spy Kids* movie," I admit. "His little brothers watched it with us, too."

"Which one?" Charity asks. "A friend of mine did some extra work on the second one, but it went straight to DVD."

I frown. "There's more than one?"

"Did he at least try to hold your hand?" Mattie asks.

"Did you hear anything I just said? We're not dating. Plus his brothers were there!"

Mattie sighs and flops back on the floor, hugging a throw cushion to her chest. "How tragic," she moans. "It's over before it even began."

"Like Romeo and Juliet," Charity adds.

"Or Bella and Jacob," Mattie sighs.

Benji giggles and I snatch the throw cushion from Mattie's arms, bopping her on the head with it. "Ugh! I can't believe you read that vampire stuff!"

"It's more than just vampire stuff," she protests. "It's a cultural phenomenon."

I roll my eyes. "Sure."

"Maybe you'll end up together, years from now," Mattie suggests.

"Stranger things have happened," Charity adds.

At first I thought it would be weird, having Charity around. She's two years older, after all. Why would she want to hang around a bunch of almost-niners? But it turns out Benji was right; she is nice. And funny. And she has great taste in movies. In fact, take her away from all those theatre kids and she's almost normal. At least as normal as Mattie is, and I hang out with her all the time.

"Or maybe he'll meet someone nicer and sweeter than me and forget all about me next year at high school."

"I doubt it," Benji says. "You're his Annie."

"His what?"

"His Annie, you know, like Doug and Annie."

Barf.

"Okay the whole star-crossed lovers thing only applies to make-believe characters, not people I have to see every day," I say. "And especially not to my mother."

"So friends, then?" Benji says.

"Friends," I agree.

"Friends is good!"

"Friends is great!"

Mattie is unconvinced. "Lovers is better," she says.

Ugh. I cover my ears. "*Must* you use that word?"

Mattie blinks. "What word would you rather I use? Partners? Significant others? Steadies?"

Mom appears at the top of the stairs. She looks fresh and pretty in a yellow and white patterned sundress, hair parted to the side, and Doug's pendant lying close to her heart. "Who's going steady?" she asks.

We answer as one, sweet, innocent voice: "No one."

235

"Where are you going?" I ask, noting her dress.

"Mini-golfing."

Doug knocks on the screen door and lets himself in, giving my mom a quick kiss on her cheek. Beside me, Mattie sighs. "I miss Andrew," she says.

"He's only been gone for two days!" I complain. "He'll be back on Monday."

"Maybe he'll bring you a present," Charity says.

"I don't think they have a gift shop at math camp," I point out.

"Clarissa, is it all right if I whisk your lovely mother away for a few hours?" Doug asks.

I pretend to think about it before answering. "I guess so."

Doug gives me a little bow. "Greatly appreciated."

Things are good between Doug and me. When I talked to him about the chair thing, he thanked me for telling him and said he completely understood where I was coming from. It didn't stop him from doling out his own particular brand of punishment, though. I have to walk Suzy after school on Mondays and Wednesdays. Sometimes Michael comes with me. It's not so bad.

"Have fun, you two!" I call after them. "Don't do anything I wouldn't do!"

"Don't worry," Doug says with a wink, "I won't break any hearts."

Benji and Mattie burst out laughing. Charity pats my shoulder.

"Ha, ha," I say sarcastically.

"I really like Doug," Mattie says as we watch them walk down the driveway, hand in hand. Mom is laughing and Doug can't stop smiling at her.

Maybe someday someone will smile at me like that. Maybe it will be Michael, or maybe it won't be. Right now I'm not that concerned. I've got Benji, Mattie, and now Charity on my side, an entire box of microwave popcorn, and pay-per-view TV to watch. School is almost over and summer is just around the corner.

Life is good.

Acknowledgements

Deepest thanks to my inspiring friends and family who continue to offer unconditional support and encouragement. Writing can only be as rich as the life lived by the writer, so thank you for enriching my life. Special thanks to everyone at Scholastic Canada, my Flying Dragon family, my dearly beloved Spaduplexers, Anne Shone, Sally Harding, Kallie George (my second pair of eyes), and Rebecca Jess (my third pair of eyes). Love, love, love.